Class No. ___J.___   Acc No. __C/88396__

Author: __Flynn, A.__   Loc: __1 - MAY 2000__

LEABHARLANN
CHONDAE AN CHABHAIN

1. This book may be kept three weeks.
   It is to be returned on / before the last date
   stamped below.
2. A fine of 20p will be charged for every week
   or part of week a book is overdue.

This Edition first published 1999 by

MENTOR PRESS
43 Furze Road,
Sandyford Industrial Estate,
Dublin 18.

Tel. (01) 295 2112/3   Fax. (01) 295 2114
e-mail: all@mentorbooks.ie

ISBN: 1-902586-59-X

A catalogue record for this book is available from the
British Library

*All the characters in this book are fictitious.
Any resemblance to actual persons, living or dead,
is purely coincidental.*

Cover Illustration: Jimmy Lawlor
Typesetting, editing, design and layout by Mentor Press
Printed in Ireland by ColourBooks

CONTENTS

The Author

Arthur Flynn

Arthur Flynn lives in Bray, County Wicklow. He is the Honorary Secretary of the Irish centre of International PEN and is the Treasurer of the Society of Irish Playwrights.

He has written a number of radio plays including *To Scare a Spook*, *Remember Me* and *Mysterious Mr Maxwell*. He also has written many children's plays for radio including the Captain Mungo series. For television he has written scripts for *Bosco*, *Wanderly Wagon*, *Fortycoats* and *The Live Mike*.

He is the author of several books including *Echoes* (1978), *Irish Dance* (1981), *History of Bray* (1986), *Irish Film: 100 Years* (1996), and his first books with Mentor, *Achill Adventure* (1997), and *Luke's Heroes* (1998).

Dedicated to Luke
who provided
much of the inspiration

1. Exam Results

With his shirt tail flying, Luke Carroll zigzagged around empty dustbins and miniature trees on his BMX.

He sped through the small estate of semi-detached houses on the outskirts of Bray, his Man United bag slung over his shoulder, like a Pony Express rider. He ran his bike onto the grass outside his house, hopped off and raced down the side passage to the back door. As usual when he reached the kitchen he flung his bag into a corner. Standing beside the table he quickly tucked into the yoghurt and milk his mother had set out. He licked the lid of the yoghurt in between gulps of milk.

Castro, his black and white cat, was curled up on the windowsill. On hearing the familiar voice he lifted his head and sprang onto the table beside Luke. The boy petted him on the head.

Before Luke had finished eating his mother entered the kitchen. She didn't look too pleased. 'Well Luke, where is it?' she enquired.

Luke screwed up his face and mumbled, 'What?'

His mother folded her arms determinedly and leaned against the washing machine. 'Don't come that with me. You know exactly what I mean,' she said in a louder voice.

Luke knew only too well what his mother was referring to but decided to put on his innocent act. It had worked before. Maybe it would again. 'Eh, do you mean my dirty football kit?'

His mother's cheeks began twitching with her growing impatience. 'I mean your school report. Surely you haven't forgotten that? It's a small sheet of paper with numbers and words on it.'

Luke's face reddened and he became flustered. 'Emm, I don't think I got one yet, I think . . .'

Mrs Carroll held out her hand and demanded, 'Now Luke, hand it over, I mean it. I know you have it. No messing around.'

Luke shrugged and shuffled over to the corner. He scrambled in his school bag and drew out a half-eaten cheese sandwich, a biro with the end chewed off and an assortment of dog-eared books. He was hoping that if he delayed long enough his mother might forget or the phone might ring but he was wrong. His mother stood over him tapping her foot.

Luke sucked in his lips as he took out a crumpled envelope from the bottom of his bag. Silently he handed it to his mother. She flattened out the envelope and removed the report. Slowly her gaze moved down the sheet, her expression growing more annoyed with every line.

Luke grew uneasy and stood upright. He shuffled his feet about and then announced quickly, 'I'm off, Mam, see you later.'

'Not so fast, young man,' she snapped grabbing his arm. 'I want a word with you . . . what have you got to say for yourself?'

'Well, I wasn't feeling the best when I did the exams . . . remember I wasn't . . .' began Luke.

His mother frowned and stood directly in front of him. She spoke in a cross voice. 'This is a deplorable report. It gets worse every time. Just look at this "easily distracted" . . . "Luke does not concentrate" . . . "his written English and vocabulary are very poor . . ."'

'I wouldn't mind that. Sure the English teacher can't stand me anyway. She's a right eejit, always going on. She'd never say anything good about me,' said Luke, trying to wriggle out of it.

His mother cut across him. 'Enough of your excuses. If you put as much effort into your schoolwork as you do football and gadding about you'd do fine. From—'

'But Mam—' he protested.

'I can assure you that you're going to get a rude awakening. I'm taking you in hand from here on,' threatened his mother.

The colour was draining out of Luke's face and he still protested, 'Ah, but Mam, I promise I'll do better from now on. I'll be extra good next year . . . really.'

'I know you will because I'm going to enrol you in drama classes. Miss Foot will teach you how to speak and behave properly. She won't have you going around like a ragbag,' explained his mother.

Luke's mouth opened in amazement, 'Ah Mam, you're having me on. Not that ol' sissy stuff. I'd die if the lads ever found out. I could always try—'

His mother cut in sharply and wagged her finger at him. 'I don't care what you think. I'm sick giving you warnings. You never take them seriously. You'll be starting with Miss Foot next Friday and that's final.'

Luke threw his arms up in despair and moaned, 'Ah, but Mam . . . you wouldn't do that to me? It's as bad as putting a bow in my hair. Is there nothing else? I'll promise anything, do anything.'

'Luke I'm warning you. If you keep this up I'm going to ground you for a week as well,' said his mother, moving away from him.

'If you did that I wouldn't be able to go to the stupid nancy drama class,' muttered Luke to himself. He kicked his school bag in temper.

Luke quickly changed into his jeans and tee shirt and left the house without speaking to his mother again. He gave a shrill whistle and called, 'Castro, Castro'. The cat came racing out the back door and sprang into the box on the rear of Luke's bike. Luke cycled to the seafront and met up with his two pals, Sticky and Damien, outside the Sea Life Aquarium. They parked their bikes against a small wall. Luke was still moody.

Luke was often known as Freckles, because they covered every inch of his face. His hair was red and cut short. He was extremely fit as he played football every spare minute. He played Gaelic on the school team and was one of their leading scorers. He played soccer with Ardmore Rovers, and on the road with his pals. His pet hate was school and he would give it up for good if he was allowed.

Sticky's real name was Kieran Nolan but he had the nickname 'Sticky' since he was a baby because he loved sweets and his fingers were always sticky. He liked sport but was more for taking things easy. He supported Liverpool and Luke, Man United. They were always having rows over who was the best team.

Damien Morgan was often called Mop because he was skinny with a mop of bushy fair hair. He was up early every morning as he had a paper round in a few estates near his house.

'What's up with you?' asked Sticky, tugging at Luke's tee shirt.

Luke shook him loose and walked on, increasing his

speed. 'Leave me alone. I'm in lousy form.'

'What's up? Is your old lady on your house again?' he enquired.

'Yeah, she never lets up,' he moaned.

'Sure mine's the same, never stops. The state of my room, my homework, clothes, you name it. She's always narking about something,' added Damien with a frown.

Sticky nodded, 'I think that's what mothers were sent down here for. To make sure we don't have a good time.'

'Ah, give over the pair of you, you're making me feel worse,' said Luke, sitting on the prom railings.

Sticky sat beside him. 'What'll we do?'

'Well I feel like something to eat,' said Luke in an effort to cheer himself up.

'Me too, but I'm skint. I couldn't even afford a tenpenny bag,' sighed Damien, leaning against the railings.

Sticky turned out his pockets and announced, 'I haven't got a sausage on me either.'

Luke, with a sly glint in his eye, ordered, 'Come on, I've got an idea.' He vaulted across the seats on the prom and headed towards a kiosk.

Damien and Sticky trotted behind him, 'What are you at now? Sure we haven't got a make between us,' asked Damien.

'Count me out if you're going to chance something dodgy. I'm off,' said Sticky in a jittery voice.

'Get lost then, you yella baby. I couldn't care less about you. Go on!' roared Luke.

'You go and distract your man in the kiosk,' instructed Luke.

Damien sighed. 'What'll I do?'

'Ask him something . . . anything,' snapped Luke.

11

Damien stood at the door of the kiosk. The old man stood up from his stool.

'Can I help you, Sonny?' he asked.

Damien became nervous. His palms became sweaty and he wiped them against the side of his jeans.

'Eh . . . emm . . . did you see around the back, mister?'

'No,' replied the man suspiciously. 'What's the matter?'

'You . . . you'd want to check it,' he stuttered, as he moved towards the rear. The man opened the half door and followed him.

'Well . . . eh . . . you see . . . all the other kiosks have signs . . .' began Damien.

When Luke heard them talking he cautiously approached the kiosk. He listened for a while as Damien waffled on. He shot his hand across the counter and grabbed a bar of chocolate. Immediately Luke tore off across the grass, followed by his two pals. He raced up a side road and took a sharp turn into a laneway. He leaned against the wall almost breathless.

The others caught up with him. 'Are . . . you . . . cracked or something?' spluttered Sticky. 'Do you know what you did?'

'It's one way to get something free when you're skint,' said Luke, with a smile.

'Are you mad? What if he calls the guards? We could be rightly in the soup,' said Damien in a worried voice.

Luke tore the wrapper off the bar and took a bite. 'You pair should be in the girl guides. Afraid to chance anything.'

'What's up with you today, Lukie? You're acting weird,' asked Damien.

Luke lowered his head. 'Ah nothing,' he muttered. There was no way he was going to tell them his problem. They had probably got no better results than he had but they weren't being sent to drama class. Even being grounded for a week wouldn't have been that bad.

2. Drama Class

Over the next week Luke did his best to put the idea of the drama class out of his mind. Within a few days he had completely forgotten about it and got on with the other exciting things in his life – football and pop music.

On Friday Luke returned from school as usual and sat down to rush through his lunch. Barbara, his sister, sat opposite him, enjoying her food at a more leisurely pace.

'What are you looking at?' Luke snapped at his sister.

'You, with your wonderful manners,' she replied sarcastically.

Their mother came in from the garden, carrying an armful of apples.

'Luke, will you slow down, before you make yourself sick,' she warned, placing an apple on the table in front of each of them.

'Ah, but Mam, the lads will be down any minute. I'll have to gallop,' he spluttered through a mouthful of yoghurt.

His mother placed her hand on his shoulder forcing him back onto the chair.

'And what may I ask is the panic?' she enquired.

'I've got a match on, it's dead important. They'll all be waiting,' he said, anxious to leave.

His mother shook her head. 'Wrong, my good man, have you forgotten what day this is?'

He pulled a face and stared at his mother. 'Eh . . . Friday . . . What's that got to do with it?'

By now Barbara was covering her mouth with her hand to hide her amusement. Her mother held up a threatening finger to her as she continued to address Luke.

'Your first drama class is on today, and you'll be there come what may.'

Luke had hoped she had forgotten her threat of a week earlier.

'Ah but Mam, you know I hate all that stuff – it's only for sissies – all dancing and speaking posh.'

'Look at that nice David Nolan, he's so mannerly and speaks so nicely. He never misses a class,' his mother said, determinedly.

Luke scoffed, 'You wouldn't mind him, he's real posh. Is that the way you want me to turn out?'

'None of that cheek,' said his mother, with her crossest face and voice. 'At least he keeps himself neat and tidy and gets good results in his exams, which is more than can be said for you'.

'And he knows how to speak properly,' jeered Barbara.

'Oul poshy boots! Who wants to go around spouting Shakespeare and all that rubbish?' retorted Luke.

'Enough of this guff,' hs mother said. 'You're going and that's that. Besides, according to Barbara, Miss Foot said that there would be a special announcement today.'

He was not impressed. 'Probably another stupid play, or poetry or some such,' he grunted.

As the argument continued there was a ring on the doorbell. Luke darted out to answer it. Damien and Sticky were bouncing a ball on the doorstep.

'Are you ready?' asked Sticky.

'I can't go,' sighed Luke, with a long face. 'My Mam says I have to . . . to do something else.'

Damien demanded, 'What's more important than football?'

Barbara sneaked up behind Luke and announced in a loud voice, 'I know why he can't go. He has to go to Miss Foot's drama class – that's where he's off to.'

'Is she serious?' asked Sticky in disbelief.

Damien screwed up his face in disgust. 'Are you out of your mind? You're going to learn to talk posh and all that rubbish. That's a laugh.'

'All that prancing around and fancy poems,' jeered Sticky. 'You can't be serious.'

Luke became embarrassed and his face reddened. 'Give over, will you, it's not my fault. It's not my idea of fun. No way do I want to go but Mam is going to ground me if I don't.'

Damien did a mock impression of a teapot and mimicked 'I'm a little teapot, short and stout.'

Sticky was hooting with laughter.

Luke's temper got the better of him and he shoved Damien off the step. 'Knock it off, you pair, give over your slagging. I'm not in the humour for it.'

'Old sarky puss,' snapped Damien. 'Can't even take a joke.'

Sticky turned his back, picked up the ball and began to walk away muttering, 'Okay, if that's the way you feel. We get the message.'

'And when you're on in the Abbey we'll come and have a gawk at you. Will you get us in for free?' jeered Damien as a parting remark, as he followed Sticky.

Luke called after them, 'Ah hang on a minute lads. I didn't mean to get ratty. The stupid class will be over at half four. I'll see you then – OK?'

'Wouldn't it be a shame to dirty your nice clean clothes playing football?' shouted Sticky back at him.

In a flaming humour, Luke slammed the door and went back inside. 'Now look what you're after doing. They'll think I'm a right sissy,' he grumbled as he walked into the kitchen.

'That's enough out of you,' said his mother.

Luke sighed. 'Let's get going then.'

'I'm glad to see you're anxious to go,' said Mrs Carroll, taking the car keys out of her handbag.

Luke nearly went wild with her remark but thought it best not to say anything else.

Luke and Barbara quickly changed out of their school uniforms and into tee shirts and jeans. They got into the car and Luke sat in the back seat sulking. Mrs Carroll drove the short distance to the Harbour View Hotel and dropped them off.

Barbara ran on ahead to catch up with two classmates. Luke hung back, tempted to slip down a laneway and do a bunk but he knew he wouldn't get away with it. Reluctantly he entered the hotel and moved like a tortoise down a long passageway to a room at the rear. Maybe the class will be cancelled, he hoped secretly, but no such luck. From inside he could hear giggling and excited chatter. Fiddling with the handle of the door, he hesitated, wondering if it wasn't too late to change his mind.

Suddenly David Nolan was standing behind him. Luke didn't like him that much. As usual David looked as if every stitch of clothes he wore was brand new, he hadn't got a hair out of place. Before Luke had time to say a word, David was holding the door open for him.

'Go ahead, Luke,' he said politely.

Luke walked into the room with his hands in his pockets and looked for a seat towards the back. Maybe they wouldn't notice him, he hoped. The children, mainly girls, were sitting in a semi-circle. In the centre stood Miss Foot who was called 'Foot by name and Foot by nature'. She was in her late fifties and was tall and thin. She wore her grey hair in a bun. Her glasses were dangling around her neck on a silver chain. She lifted the glasses to her eyes to see who the newcomer was.

'Oh Luke, how nice of you to grace us with your presence,' she said in her high-pitched voice. 'Children, this is our new pupil, Luke Carroll. I want you all to make him welcome.'

Luke didn't reply. He merely blushed and lowered his eyes.

'You can sit there,' she said, pointing her purple nail-varnished finger at a chair directly in front of her.

As he quickly shuffled onto the chair, he could hear some girls to his right tittering. He was positive Barbara was one of them but he dared not look.

'Enough of the jollities, let's get down to some real work,' instructed Miss Foot, clapping her hands dramatically.

There was instant silence from all the children. Miss Foot flicked through the pages of her book and glanced around at the faces.

Luke lowered his head to make sure she wouldn't single him out. He gave a sigh of relief when she didn't call his name but called his sister instead.

'Barbara, would you say your piece please?'

Barbara stood with a smug expression and began to recite in her best voice, 'If I was a lady'.

By the third line Luke was bored stiff. He had heard this recitation over and over at home. He knew every word and every action. Any kind of punishment would have been better than going to these boring classes. He didn't want to be an actor or a poet. He didn't want to speak posh. His pals would only slag him. If he had his way, he would run a mile from this and spend all his time playing football or in the amusement arcade. His big dream was to play international soccer for Ireland. He could see himself running onto the pitch in the green jersey like Paul McGrath and scoring the winning goal.

He daydreamed his way through the poems and recitations of several girls with names like Serena, Vicky and Majella. They all sounded the same to him.

There was only one thing that amused him during the entire class. It was Miss Foot's habit of licking her finger and running it along her eyebrow. Luke couldn't help smirking behind his hand every time he saw her doing it.

His daydreaming was abruptly disturbed when Miss Foot again clapped her hands and called for order.

'Now listen children as I promised last week I have something special to tell you'.

There were 'oohs' and 'aahs' as everybody, including Luke, paid attention.

'A producer from Ardmore Studios has been in touch with me about a new film which will be shot in County Wicklow in a few weeks time. They are looking for several children to play parts in this film and they would like you all to go up to the studios for auditions,' explained Miss Foot.

She was interrupted by a string of questions.

'Are we all going to be in the film?'

'Is it a dancing film?'

'Is Meryl Streep in it?'

'Will we be paid a mint?'

'Will we have talking parts?'

'Do they need good soccer players?' Luke was surprised to hear himself asking.

Another loud clap and a stamp of her foot brought silence again. 'The answer to all these questions is, I don't know,' she began. 'All they told me is that they would like to audition all of you. This could be the big opportunity for some of you. Just look at Shirley Temple'.

'Who is she?' asked someone.

Miss Foot rolled her eyes to heaven. 'Only the most successful child actor ever. Never mind—'

The excited chatter soon drowned her voice out as they discussed this news.

David Nolan grinned at Luke. 'Do you fancy being a film star?' he asked.

Luke shrugged. 'I wouldn't mind, but I'd prefer to be a footballer.'

'Actors make far more money,' said David.

'How would you know, you never kicked a ball in your life. Probably afraid to dirty your nice clean shoes,' said Luke, turning his back on him.

'But you have never asked me to play with you,' replied David very quietly.

Luke knew this was true, they had always assumed that David couldn't or wouldn't play but before he had time to reply, Miss Foot called the class to order. 'You are all very restless and giddy today, maybe I should cancel the trip to the studio.'

'Ah no, Miss,' cried Barbara and some other girls.

'We'll be good, we'll be good.'

Miss Foot's glossy red lips parted and she smiled. 'Oh very well. Now children I have a note for your parents giving the details. For those of you who are allowed to go, I want you to meet at my house next Friday at 3.30pm. There will be a mini-bus to take you to the studio.'

This was greeted by a loud cheer and stamping of feet.

3. David's Skill

Luke daydreamed throughout the remainder of the class and didn't hear a word that was spoken. Maybe the film might be fun after all, he thought, so long as he didn't have to recite poetry or get dressed up like a dog's dinner or make an eejit of himself.

The other children were filing out of the room before Luke realised that the class had been dismissed.

'You must like it here, do you want to stay for the night?' asked David, pulling Luke by the sleeve.

Luke wriggled free and made for the door. He zigzagged through the other children as they made their way along the passageway and out onto the street. He turned on hearing a sharp whistle and his name being called.

Across the road Sticky was sitting on his BMX and Damien was bouncing a ball against the wall, his bike was lying on the footpath.

'So you couldn't do without me,' shouted Luke.

'We wanted to see if you would be any different after all the drama,' jeered Damien.

'It would have been a dead loss trying to play a match without our best player,' shouted Sticky.

'Thanks a lot. Hey, wait till I tell you the news,' began Luke excitedly.

'Oh spare us. We don't want to hear about corny poetry and all that drama stuff,' spat Sticky.

'I've got a better idea,' said Damien spotting David Nolan and running off to intercept him. .

The other two stood looking puzzled.

'What's Mop up to?' asked Sticky.

Luke shook his head. 'I haven't got a clue. Sure, he's always going off with some hair-brained idea.'

They caught up with Damien as he reached David. 'Hey David, do you fancy a game of footy?'

David's mouth opened in astonishment. 'You're not having me on, are you?' he asked warily.

Damien kept a straight face. 'No, no. I'm on the level. We're just going to have a bit of a kick around.'

'Oh great, I'd love to,' he replied, his face brightening up. 'But I haven't got any gear with me.'

'That doesn't matter, it's not the World Cup. You'll be all right as you are,' replied Damien, heading towards the seafront.

Luke gripped Damien by the arm and muttered. 'Are you out of your mind, or what? He can't play!'

Damien winked mischievously. 'Let's see how good he is. What's the betting that he goes home whingeing to his mammy?'

Luke gave a sly smile and whispered. 'I get the idea. He wants to play so let's see how good he is.'

The boys continued on over the level crossing and onto the green stretch, which ran parallel with the promenade. Sticky rested his bicycle against a sign which read 'NO CYCLING OR FOOTBALL'.

Sticky whipped off his pullover and threw it in a heap on the grass as a makeshift goalpost. Then he paced out ten steps for the goalmouth. 'Let's have another jumper,' he called.

'Sure! You can have mine,' said David, quickly volunteering. He pulled off his pullover and dropped it at Sticky's feet.

'Who's going to be the goalie?' asked Damien.

'What about David?' replied Luke.

David seemed pleased and said, 'I don't mind. I'll give it a try.'

'Right lads, let's get started,' snapped Damien, bouncing the ball. He beckoned Sticky and Luke forward. They went into a huddle. 'Let him have it from all sides.'

'This should be gas,' chuckled Luke.

They fanned out and Damien passed the ball to Sticky, he dribbled it along the ground, showing off his fancy footwork. David stood midway between the pullovers in a crouched position, his hands outstretched. He kept his eye on the ball as it passed between them. Then Sticky took a hard slug at the ball and it swirled towards the goal. David leapt forward and blocked the ball with his chest and hands and fell to the ground clutching it.

The others stared at him in amazement.

'Are my eyes deceiving me, or did he really stop it?' blurted Damien.

'It was probably only a fluke catch,' said Sticky with a shrug.

'Let's try him again so,' said Luke walking backwards.

'You'll have to do better than that if you want to get one past me,' smiled David as he kicked the ball out of his hands.

Luke sprang forward, not waiting for the ball to land and lobbed it directly back at him. David took a plunge and landed on the ball, preventing the goal. The knees of his trousers were dusty now and there was a grass stain on the front of his tee shirt.

Sticky became annoyed. 'You never told us he was this good.'

Damien lowered his head and whispered. 'How the hell was I to know? I don't knock around with him. I thought he was a dead loss. I didn't think he knew the sideline from the goalpost.'

Luke kicked the grass in bad temper. 'He's making a right eejit out of us. That's two he's after saving.'

'Ah, don't lose your cool, lads. I'm not really that good. Don't give up yet,' laughed David, as he stood up and brushed the dust off his clothes.

After David had saved a third and fourth goal, Luke decided he had had enough humiliation for one day. 'Tell you what, it's about time we packed it up. I'm starving.'

'That was deadly lads. Can we play again?' asked David, looking extremely happy.

The lads exchanged glances. None of them were keen to play with him again but they said nothing.

'I'd better push off,' said David, as they began to move away. 'See you around.'

Luke waited until David was out of earshot and commented. 'My God, he's not half bad, is he?'

'Forget about him. Did you hear the news about what's coming to the town?' Damien asked excitedly.

'No. What?' said Luke in a couldn't-care-less attitude.

'Go on, have a guess.'

Luke tossed out a few names. 'Oasis . . . The Pope . . . whoever.'

Sticky shook his head. 'I haven't got a clue. Tell us.'

Damien gave a broad grin. 'It's the Tour de France.'

Luke sniggered. 'Will you give over. Who are you trying to cod? The Tour de France.'

'Honest to God. Cross my heart and hope to die,' said Damien making a sign of the cross over his heart.

'You don't expect us to fall for that one?' said Sticky in disbelief.

'Straight up. My da told me,' replied Damien.

'He must be as big a liar as you are. Tour de France, my foot!' jeered Sticky.

'I'd lay you a thousand to one it's not on,' said Luke with assurance.

'No way, Damo. Sure it's only on in France,' added Sticky, not at all convinced.

'I don't care what you say. It's definitely on. You'll see,' said Damien in a loud voice.

'But what's it coming to Bray for?' asked Sticky.

'If you said today is Friday I wouldn't believe you,' said Luke, scoffing.

'Come on then.' Damien was determined.

'Where are you off to?' enquired Luke.

'Up to my house. My da will tell you. You'll see,' said Damien.

'Are you mad or something?' said Sticky.

'Just belt up and come on,' retorted Damien, getting more annoyed by the minute.

They stopped arguing. Luke hopped onto the back of Sticky's bike and they followed their friend up the town. Damien pushed down hard on the pedals, feeling betrayed by their disbelief. When he rounded the corner into his road, he was relieved to see his father's car in the driveway. He flung his bike onto the ground and pushed in the hall door. Seconds later he returned, followed by his father.

'Da, you tell them what's coming to Bray in July. Go on,' he demanded.

His father smiled as he replied, 'You mean the Tour

de France, son?'

Damien waved his finger at them. 'That shook you. Now who's right? Didn't I tell you?'

'Is that straight up, Mr Morgan?' asked Luke.

'I'm glad to say it is. On the the twelfth of July the Tour de France will be coming right up the Main Street,' replied Mr Morgan.

Sticky scratched his head. He couldn't figure it out. 'Why, are they lost, or something?'

They all burst out laughing.

'You're a right dingbat,' jeered Luke, pulling his ear.

Mr Morgan looked at his watch and said 'Sorry lads, if that's all, I'll have to be off'.

'Good luck, Mr Morgan,' said Luke as he moved away from the door.

'There. Didn't I tell you? It's going to be deadly,' grinned Damien.

'We could be on the telly,' said Sticky, throwing up his hands.

'Will you give over. Anyone would think you were riding in the flippin' race yourself,' laughed Luke.

4. The Audition

The main topic of discussion in the Carroll house during the evening meal was the audition for the film Miss Foot had spoken about.

'I hope it's one of those lovely romantic films like *Little Women* and that we get to wear beautiful long dresses,' said Barbara in a dreamy voice.

Luke sniggered. 'If they're looking for little women they'll have a right one with you.'

His mother waved her finger at him. 'Less of that talk now, Luke. If they're looking for a scruffy young fellow you'll fit the bill perfectly.'

'Mam, how much do you think we'll get?' asked Barbara.

Her mother smiled. 'According to this notice, you're all only going for an audition. Nothing might come of it, so don't go building your hopes up.'

Barbara was disappointed. 'How do you mean, nothing might come of it? I thought we were all going to be in the film.'

'No Barbara, people go for auditions all the time, even the big time stars, but the film makers only pick the people they want,' she explained.

Luke stuffed his mouth with chips as he asked, 'Tell us, what are auditions, what do we have to do?'

'You're a right eejit, sure everybody knows that,' laughed Barbara.

'Tell us then, smarty pants, if you know it all,' demanded Luke.

'It's when people have to do their act before the

director and he picks out the best one! Isn't that right, Mam?' said Barbara boastfully.

'Dead right, Barbara,' said her mother, patting her on the head.

Luke scratched his head and looked puzzled. 'You mean it's a sort of competition – do we have to sing or dance?'

'No, they will probably only take a look at you, and if they like you they'll take you on,' explained his mother doing her best to make it clear.

Barbara burst out laughing. 'With a face like his he would only get the part of a space monster or a pig from *Animal Farm*.

'Look who's talking – your face would make a spider look beautiful,' mocked Luke.

Their mother clapped her hands. 'Enough of this carry on, or I won't let either of you go,' she said crossly.

'You mean we can go then?' asked Barbara.

'I don't see why not. Just as long as it doesn't interfere with your schooling,' said Mrs Carroll as she divided out a tin of fruit between them.

'Oh, great. Will you iron my good dress and help me to do my hair?' said Barbara, gulping down her tea.

'What can I wear?' grunted Luke.

His mother shrugged. 'That's up to you, everything you own is either torn or stained.'

Barbara sent out a spray of food as she giggled. 'Sure the only things he has that are half decent are his pyjamas.'

'Ha, ha, very funny,' said Luke.

As the days went by Luke began to look forward to going up to the studios. He had lived in Bray all his life and had driven past Ardmore Studios many times but he had never been inside the gate. There were uniformed security men in an office at the entrance and he had often wondered what kind of amazing things they were guarding. Would there be spaceships and guns and tanks? Sticky had told them that a man his father knew said that there was a replica of an entire French street built in the grounds. On Friday he hoped to find out for himself.

Luke, Barbara and the rest of the children gathered at Miss Foot's house on Friday at 3.30pm as arranged. The girls were far cleaner than the boys with their new dresses and their hair in ringlets and curls. Most of the boys wore shirts, ties and pants. Luke was the only one wearing his tee shirt and jeans.

Miss Foot walked among the children, straightening a bow or brushing hair from a shoulder here and there. She gave a deep sigh when she came to Luke. 'My, my. Just look at the state of you. I've got a good mind not to let you go at all.'

Luke stood up to her. 'But Miss, you never said what to wear. Anyway these are my best clothes.'

She shook her head impatiently. 'Grant me patience. Why can't you follow your sister's example?'

The other children ran chattering to the window when the mini-bus drew up outside. Despite her cries for calm, the children bustled through the hall door and bundled onto the bus.

'Along with you,' ordered Miss Foot as she ushered Luke ahead of her.

He sprinted out the door and onto the mini-bus. He sat beside David Nolan on the back row.

'Isn't this exciting?' said David with a broad grin.

'Suppose so,' replied Luke, still unsure whether he

liked the idea or not. It was too late now to change his mind as they were soon on their way. He'd better make the most of it. David yapped all the way, but Luke didn't hear a word he was saying.

Luke felt butterflies in his stomach as the security man waved them through the gates. Pressing his face against the window he saw enormous buildings with STAGE A and STAGE B on the doors. There were names on other doors too – DRESSING ROOMS, PROPS, PRODUCTION OFFICE, MAKE-UP, SPECIAL EFFECTS. He scrutinised every face they passed in case it might be a famous film star, but he didn't recognise anyone.

The mini-bus stopped in the car park and the children climbed out. Miss Foot led them towards STAGE C. Luke lagged behind, fascinated by the surroundings. He kept hoping he would see James Bond's car or a knight on a charger or at least a clown or something exotic.

'Luke Carroll, don't be so nosy. And hurry up,' barked Miss Foot.

Luke ran to catch up with the others as they entered STAGE C. A small man with a ponytail and dressed in jeans, a white tee shirt and a leather waistcoat spoke to them, 'And who have we got here?' he enquired in an English accent.

'The Gladys Foot School of Acting!' announced Miss Foot proudly.

Miss Foot and the man spoke for a few minutes and then he led the children to the top of the large stage. Rows of chairs were set out facing a long table. There was a grey-haired man and two younger women sitting behind the table.

Miss Foot organised the children into single file and addressed them, 'Now heads up and be on your best behaviour. When you get the signal, walk to the centre of the table and say your name. Clearly! Then wait.'

Luke felt nervous as he watched the first two girls walk out and speak. He licked his lips and wiped his sweaty palms on the side of his jeans. He was beginning to regret that he had come. His head was pounding, but none of the others seemed to be a bit bothered.

'Next,' called one of the women.

Nobody moved. Luke felt all eyes turning to him. Suddenly a sharp finger dug him in the back.

'That's you,' hissed Miss Foot.

Luke lunged forward to the centre of the table. He nibbled nervously on his lower lip as he waited.

'Name?' asked the same woman.

'Lu – Lu – Luke Carroll,' he stuttered.

'Age?' she enquired.

'Emm . . . eh. . . eleven,' he replied.

The man looked him up and down. 'How fit are you?'

Luke shrugged. 'Emm . . . all right, I suppose.'

'Do you swim . . . play football . . . or engage in any sport?' enquired the second woman.

Luke nodded. 'Oh yeah, I'm game for anything – everything.'

'Would you turn around please?' instructed the first woman.

Luke was puzzled. What's going on here, he wondered? He did as she asked, then stood still. He could hear whispering behind his back.

After a while a female voice said, 'Thanks Luke, you can go now.'

As he turned to leave a man's voice called him from the right. 'Over here.'

Luke spun round to see a photographer pointing towards a wall and beckoning him to stand there. Reluctantly Luke complied, uncertain what to expect.

'Ready?' asked the photographer.

'Yeah,' grunted Luke, feeling like a criminal in a line-up.

He hated having his photograph taken. In all the snaps in the family album Luke was either in a sulk or pulling a funny face. This time was no different and Luke scowled as the bulb flashed.

When all the children were finished, Miss Foot led them outside. She immediately drew Luke aside.

'Trust you, Luke Carroll. You let us down dreadfully. The sour puss on you, anyone would imagine you were going to the dentist.'

'How was I supposed to know? Nobody told me I had to smile,' he replied brazenly.

Miss Foot turned her eyes to the sky. 'Grant me patience, you'll never learn.'

Luke didn't need to be told that he had not made a good impression but it didn't bother him. He realised his career in the movie world would be a short one. It was no big deal; he had packs of other things to do. If it had been a photograph for a football team he would have smiled from ear to ear.

The children all returned to the mini-bus and chatted excitedly about the experience. Luke sat quietly and didn't hear a word that David Nolan was saying to him.

Back home Luke's mother greeted him and Barbara at the door anxious to hear how they had got on. Immediately

Barbara burst into a flow of words giving every detail of the outing to the studio.

'It was wonderful, Mam. They were all so nice to us. Everything was colossal up there.'

Her mother waited until Barbara took a breath and then turned to Luke.

'And what about you, Luke? How did you get on?'

'Emm, OK, I suppose. They only asked me my name and then took a photo. It was all a waste of time, I suppose, as far as I'm concerned,' he groaned.

His mother wasn't surprised, she knew Luke of old.

Luke went to his room and switched on FM104 and turned up the volume full blast. The room throbbed with the beat. After a while his mother appeared at his bedroom door with a brush, dustpan and black sack in her hand.

'Right, Luke, I mean business,' she said determinedly. 'For a start, turn down that racket, I can't hear myself think.'

Luke reluctantly crawled off his bed and turned down the volume. 'Ah Mam,' he protested.

His mother surveyed the room. There were heaps of jeans, tee shirts, dirty socks, and empty Coke cans, Mars bars and chewing gum wrappers. There were CD covers, football magazines and torn posters strewn around the floor.

'Luke, you have made about fifty promises. Your room is a bombsite. It's a health hazard. This is D-Day.'

Luke dived onto the floor grabbing a pair of jeans and a Manchester United magazine.

'Cross my heart, Mam, I'll do it right from now on. You'll only go throwing out all my good things.'

'You must be joking. War on Want wouldn't accept a

single item from this room. Anything you don't hang up is going in the bag. You have half an hour to do it and I'll be back to check. There'll be no mercy this time,' she stressed, handing him the black sack.

Luke rolled onto his back as she closed the door behind her. He glanced around the room, not having a clue where to start. He got up off the floor and began by putting the Coke cans and wrappers into the sack. Then his eyes opened wide. Was he seeing things? No, it was for real! There was his gift voucher for Golden Discs. His godmother had given it to him for Christmas and it had been missing ever since. He swore that Barbara had pinched it. There had been a hell of a row, with yelling and hair pulling, when he had accused her. He had been grounded for a week.

He examined the voucher closely. It was for twenty pounds. Just enough to get the new CD by Robbie Williams. Maybe cleaning his room wasn't such a bad idea after all. He smiled to himself as he tidied a bit more. Maybe he would find other long-lost goodies. He still didn't fancy the tidying bit, so when he failed to discover any other valuables he decided to slip out and head for the record shop. If he was quiet enough he could be out and back before his mother missed him.

Luke zipped up his tracksuit top and put the gift voucher in his pocket. He tiptoed across the landing and down the stairs. He bit his lip as he eased open the hall door and closed it behind him. He decided against taking his bike and broke into a sprint. Out along Killarney Road he ran, weaving in and out around the pedestrians. Within minutes he reached Golden Discs. He knew exactly where the Robbie Williams CDs were, as he had endlessly inspected them. He handed over the voucher; the precious CD was his.

He left the shop feeling like a million dollars. This had been a real bonus. He wouldn't mind cleaning his room if he could listen to Robbie Williams. As he headed back up the Main Street, he heard a car horn sounding. He ignored it, but then there was a second, louder blast. He turned towards the traffic to see Miss Foot waving frantically at him from her car. Luke gave a friendly wave and continued walking.

Miss Foot gave another blast and leaned over to open the passenger door.

'Get in,' she ordered.

Luke felt his face redden as he quickly slipped into the passenger seat and the car drove away. Surely they haven't missed me already, he thought. They couldn't have organised a search party this quickly.

'Are you daydreaming or something? Did you not hear me calling you?' she snapped, giving him one of her infamous stares.

'I didn't know—'

'Never mind all that,' she said with a wave of her hand. 'I was on my way to your house anyway.'

'Oh—' began Luke, assuming he was in trouble.

Miss Foot didn't speak to him again, but drove to the Carroll house. Luke nibbled his lip as he tried to think up an excuse. What could he have done? Surely it wasn't for messing in class or in the studio?

Mrs Carroll came to the hall door on hearing the car parking in the driveway. She smiled at Miss Foot and then glared at Luke.

'What's he done this time?' she asked sharply.

36

'Oh nothing,' beamed Miss Foot, 'quite the opposite.'

Luke was baffled but his curiosity was soon satisfied.

'I can't imagine why but the film company want to use Luke in their movie,' announced Miss Foot.

Luke's mother struggled for words.

'You mean . . . he . . . are you sure?'

'I'm afraid so. It just so happens that Luke has the kind of face that they want.'

'But what about Barbara?' Mrs Carroll asked.

Miss Foot shook her head.

'She's too pretty and well-groomed for this film. An "undernourished look" is exactly what they said.' Miss Foot grimaced as she spoke the words.

Luke took the opportunity to butt in. 'What will I have to do? Will I miss school? Will they give me a big limo and all?'

'Don't get any fancy notions, young man. You're only an extra, nothing more.' Miss Foot had seen it all before.

'Oh . . .' exclaimed Luke, not sure what the word 'extra' meant.

'They would have taken half a dozen more like him – if I had them,' explained Miss Foot with disgust. 'None of the well-groomed, well-spoken pupils like David Nolan were chosen.'

'That's our Luke,' smiled his mother. He could see she was very pleased. 'What happens next?' she asked Miss Foot.

'He has to go to the studio tomorrow afternoon for a fitting. Is that all right?'

'He'll be there spic-and-span,' replied his mother, tousling her son's hair.

'Not too tidy, mind you,' said Miss Foot.

'Thank you very much, Miss Foot. It was good of you to call,' said Mrs Carroll as she saw her to the door.

'Phew,' Luke sighed, as he walked inside and petted Castro.

'Well done, Luke. I never thought I'd see the day. You're going to be in the films. That's more than I've ever done,' remarked his mother walking into the kitchen. She opened her purse and produced a five pound note.

'That's for me? Deadly,' he yelled with delight as he snatched the fiver. 'When I make my first million I'll pay you back.'

'Thanks a lot,' laughed his mother.

'I won't be in for tea, I'm going to McDonalds,' he called back to her.

'Where else? Don't be late,' she said, her voice trailing after him.

5. The Fitting

Luke connected up with Damien and Sticky in McDonalds and enthusiastically told them about how he was going to be an 'extra'.

'I'd do anything to be in a film,' said Sticky, longingly.

'Yeah, me too,' added Damien.

'Would you go as far as poetry classes with girls?' giggled Luke.

'Can you get me in the film too?' asked Damien.

As he finished his Big Mac, Luke leaned forward and glanced over his shoulder to make sure nobody could hear before speaking.

'Listen I've got an idea and it might just work.'

Sticky pulled a face. 'I'm not too sure about your bright ideas. You've walked us into trouble before.'

'And just think about that stunt at the kiosk. If the guards had spotted us we would have been rightly in the soup,' complained Damien.

Luke thumped the table, annoyed. 'Right, right. If that's the way you feel about it, I won't bother telling you. You can clear off.'

'Don't mind him, Luke, he's always cribbing,' said Sticky, anxious to hear the plan.

'Right then,' began Luke. 'I was thinking that I might be able to get you pair into the film as well.'

'You're having us on,' exclaimed Sticky. 'Tell us how.'

'How could you swing something like that?' enquired Damien.

'I'm trying to tell you, if you'd only belt up and let me finish. Well, according to Miss Foot they picked me because I was skinny, scruffy and grumpy looking. Now if they thought I'm grumpy looking they should get a squint at you two,' continued Luke.

'Hey knock it off,' snapped Sticky in an angry voice. 'You're no oil painting yourself.'

Damien wasn't so put out. 'You mean we could get picked too?' he asked excitedly.

Luke shook his head. 'I didn't say that exactly but if you're game I could try something. Are you on?'

Damien scratched his chin. 'Sure there's nothing to lose. I'm in.'

'And what about you?' asked Luke, nodding towards Sticky.

'Fair enough.'

'Right, keep nix while I make a call,' ordered Luke unfolding a piece of paper from his pocket. He went to the public callbox, picked up the phone and dialled a number. Damien and Sticky followed him.

Damien was anxious. 'What are you at?'

'Shush,' muttered Luke. 'Eh . . . oh yeah . . . I'm ringing from the Gladys Foot School of Acting . . . emm . . . we believe that you are looking for more boys for your film . . . yeah . . . yeah . . . there are two other lads who might be suitable . . . they were sick on the day of the audition. Can I send them up to meet you? Their names . . . Stic . . . I mean Kieran Nolan and Damien Morgan . . . right . . . what time? OK . . . Thanks a lot.'

Luke hung up the receiver looking very pleased with himself. His two pals exchanged glances.

'Well?' demanded Damien.

'Are we in? Don't keep us in suspense,' demanded Sticky

'Could be,' teased Luke. 'You're to go to have your photos taken tomorrow afternoon.'

Damien threw a punch into the air and roared. 'Yeah! We'll be in the big dosh now.'

Sticky was more suspicious. 'You're not having us on again, are you?'

Luke dismissed him with a wave of his hand. 'I don't give a fiddlers what you think. It's up to you. I've got nothing to lose.'

'Come on, Luke, I didn't mean it like that. I'll go.'

Luke danced about with an imaginary gun shooting all around him. 'Maybe it'll be like *Star Wars* or *Die Hard*.'

By now Sticky had become excited. 'I'm dying to go. I can't wait. Just think, we're going to be movie stars.'

Damien threw back his head and laughed. 'It didn't take you long to change your mind.'

Next afternoon Luke, Damien and Sticky walked briskly up Killarney Road. They were dressed in their best trainers, jeans and tee shirts. This was to be their big day. They were heading for Ardmore Studios and stardom. Their parents had even allowed them to take a half-day from school.

'Do you know what the score is here?' asked Sticky as they approached the security man at the gate.

'I haven't got a clue what to say,' said Luke. 'We'll see what he says.'The security man stepped forward. 'What are your names?' he asked.

'I'm Luke Carroll.'

'I'm Kieran Nolan.'

'Damien Morgan.'

He checked his list and directed Luke to wardrobe and the others to the production office.

'Now remember to have a sour puss on you,' called Luke.

Damien gave a thumbs-up sign.

'See you back here,' said Luke as he popped his head into a door marked 'WARDROBE'. He couldn't see anyone inside. There were rails and rails of suits, costumes and dresses. Cautiously he walked into the building.

'You must be Luke,' he heard an Englishwoman's voice from behind a rail of clothes.

He spun round to see a smiling, tubby woman sitting on a stool. She was wearing layers of colourful material which reached down to her ankles.

'Let's see what we can do for you,' she said, sizing him up and down.

She moved down a rail checking various costumes. Finally she called to Luke. 'Let's see how you look in this. It should be about your size.'

He took the coat hanger with what appeared to be a collection of rags from her. He glared at it bewildered.

'You want me to wear these?'

She smiled at him. 'I'm afraid so, Luke. That was the height of fashion for orphans in the nineteenth century. You can try them on over there.'

With his face reddening more by the second, Luke moved into a small curtained-off cubicle. He examined the rags more closely. Was she having him on or was she serious? He hung the hanger on a hook and peeled off his tee shirt. Holding up the shabby brown worsted top, he took a deep breath before slipping it over his head. It felt itchy. He looked from side to side to make sure nobody was watching as he opened the buckle of his jeans. Quickly he took them off and pulled on the raggedy trousers. They only reached his knees. He spun around to inspect himself in the long mirror. He was mortified and looked worse than the scruffiest beggar he had ever seen. No way was he having this. It didn't matter how much money he was going to earn. His embarrassment was interrupted by a question from the woman.

'How are you making out, Luke?'

Luke was too shocked to reply. He stood stock still until she came over to him. She tried to conceal a smile.

'Fits you like a glove. Anyone would think you wore it every day.'

'I . . . I . . . can't . . .' he began.

She patted him affectionately on the shoulder. 'You'll do fine. Change back into your own clothes.'

Luke didn't need a second invitation and pulled off the top. As he was changing he heard two familiar voices in the distance. It was Sticky and Damien. The people in the production office must have liked the look of them and sent them to the wardrobe department.

'Just wait till you see the state of these two,' remarked Luke to the Englishwoman as he brushed past them and headed outside. He sat on the bumper of a truck enjoying the sun. He closed his eyes and rested his head against a wall.

After a few minutes an approaching car interrupted his rest.

It was a big black stretch limo. Luke sat upright. The only time he had seen one before was when it had collected his family to go to his granny's funeral. His mouth opened wide as the limo glided by and stopped about twenty yards from him. He stared at it, his heart pounding. Maybe there was a film star in it. Could it be Jim Carrey or Tom Hanks or even Mel Gibson?

The chauffeur stepped out of the car and opened the rear door. Luke felt the tension swelling inside him as he waited. Then out stepped Todd Harper. Was it really the American child star he had seen in loads of films . . . *Teen Adventure* . . . *To Scare a Spook* . . . *Captain Mungo*. Luke had seen all his films. Todd quickly disappeared into a building.

Luke was still staring at the limo when Sticky and Damien emerged from the wardrobe department.

'You'll never guess who I've just seen,' said Luke still astonished.

'The Spice Girls,' chuckled Sticky.

'Ah give over. I'm serious. It was Todd Harper,' stated Luke.

'No way,' said Damien. 'Sure he lives in America.'

'I swear, cross my heart,' said Luke.

'He's right you know,' came a voice from behind them. 'It was Todd Harper. He's the star of the film,' explained the wardrobe woman.

'You're not serious,' they all said in unison.

She smiled. 'He's playing the lead role. He's also an orphan like you.'

'Will we get to see him every day?' asked Luke, his eyes opening wide.

The boys couldn't wait to get back to Luke's house to tease Barbara with the news.

That evening over tea, Barbara was unable to contain her curiosity.

'You'll actually get to meet Todd Harper? He's cool. Can I come up too?' she asked longingly.

'No way. It's only for us,' gloated Luke.

Barbara was very disappointed. 'Will you try and get me his autograph . . . please?'

Luke smirked. 'I'll consider it. What's it worth?'

'Emm . . .' she began, 'two CDs.'

'No way. Are you kidding?' said Luke. 'Throw in those two posters of Blur and I might.'

Barbara sighed and mumbled. 'Oh all right then. And . . . any chance of getting me a photograph?'

'Give it a rest, will you. What do you take me for?' snapped Luke.

Over the next few days Luke, Damien and Sticky talked about nothing else but the film. They had a countdown marked on the wall of their den. Filming was to begin in the first week of their summer holidays. It was going to be the highlight of their lives. They imagined all sorts of things that might happen, from riding horses to doings stunts to fighting in battles. Barbara was envious of them but tried not to show it.

Two weeks later, Luke, Sticky and Damien got a call from the film company. They were to report to the studio to have their hair cut. This didn't seem like a big deal. On the last day of school the boys got a half-day. Charging out the school gates with shouts of delight they headed up to the studio and were brought to where the barber was working. They sat on a bench waiting to be called.

'Sure my hair's grand as it is,' remarked Damien.

'Don't be such a moan. I'll go in first,' volunteered Luke.

The door to the barber's opened and a bald man walked out rubbing his scalp. The boys sniggered.

The man glared at them. 'You won't think it's so

funny in a few minutes,' he said gruffly.

While the boys exchanged puzzled glances there was a call 'Next!' Hesitantly Luke stood up and entered the room.

'Just sit there,' instructed the barber, indicating the swivel chair.

Luke nervously sat down. The barber tied a white sheet around his neck, then silently he ran his blade over the boy's head. Luke wanted to protest but was too scared to speak. Within minutes he was left with a skinhead cut. The barber removed the sheet and shook all the cut hair to the ground. Luke stood up and caught his reflection in the mirror. It was dire. Slowly Luke walked out of the room and was too shocked to speak to his pals.

'Next!' called the barber. Reluctantly Sticky went into the room for a similar cut and was soon followed by Damien.

The three boys felt totally depressed as they walked home from the studio. This was the worst day of their lives. How could they face anybody they knew?

6. Orphans

Mr Carroll had set the alarm for six o'clock on the Monday morning. Luke didn't need an alarm clock; he had been awake for hours before it sounded.

Normally Luke hated getting up early especially when he was on his summer holidays but this was special. This was going to be different. This was going to be a great big adventure.

By five past six Luke was out of bed, dressed, washed and downstairs. His parents were both up too. It was even too early for Castro, who stayed asleep in his basket.

'Now remember, Luke, you're to be on your best behaviour. No messing around. Do you hear me?' warned his mother, as they sat down to breakfast.

'Ah Mam, don't start. What do you take me for? I won't do anything silly,' said Luke in an innocent voice.

His mother raised her eyebrows. 'Will you get off the stage, Luke Carroll. Who are you kidding? You're the biggest messer God put on the face of the earth.'

Luke sighed and said nothing. He wasn't in the mood for a lecture or an arguement at this hour of the morning. Gulping down his cornflakes and tea he headed for the hall door. He nipped in and out of the doorway, impatiently looking up and down the street until Sticky and Damien arrived in their best jeans and tee shirts.

Mr Carroll reversed the car out of the driveway and the three lads clambered in. Luke's mother was still waving her arms and giving advice from the garden gate as the car drew away. The boys chattered excitedly on the short drive to Ardmore Studios. At the studio gate they bounced out of the car without a single word of thanks.

Miss Foot stood stony faced in the centre of a group of boys anxiously looking at her watch. 'Oh, you decided to afford us the pleasure of your company at last,' she grunted.

Luke looked surprised and muttered under his breath, 'Damn, I wasn't expecting to see her.'

'Everybody's here now, follow me,' she ordered as she led them past the studio buildings. They entered the huge door of STAGE C. Inside, about thirty other boys were sitting at long trestle tables. They were met by a young man in a green sweatshirt and dyed-blonde hair. He was holding a clipboard and megaphone.

'Will you all take a seat, please,' he instructed in a Scottish accent.

The new arrivals scrambled for the spare seats and glanced around. The man addressed them. 'My name's Tommy and I'm the assistant director. I'll be looking after you boys. First some details. The film is called *Orphans' Retreat* and is set in the middle of the nineteenth century. You are all playing the part of orphans and when the orphanage is burned down you have to trek over the mountains in the winter.'

'Is he out of his tree? No way am I doing something like that,' whispered Luke holding his hand to his mouth.

'Are you all listening?' asked Tommy in a louder voice, glaring directly at Luke. 'The star of the film is Todd Harper. I'm sure you've all heard of him? Now for some important details you must all remember. Under no circumstances is anyone to talk to Todd, ask him for an autograph or take his photograph. Anyone who attempts to do so will be removed from the film immediately. Do I make myself clear? There will be no second chances.'

'He doesn't half fancy himself,' grunted Sticky. 'He's worse than ol' Breandie at school.'

Damien pulled a face. 'And I always thought Todd Harper was one of the goodies.'

'I don't think I'm going to like this caper after all. Rules and regulations. Let's hope they don't give us homework,' moaned Luke.

Tommy spoke to them again. 'You can all go now and get tea or coffee and a roll. Then down to wardrobe, into your costumes and back up here fast. Any questions?'

With no questions there was a sudden beeline for the tea counter. Luke elbowed himself to the front of the queue. He poured a cup of tea and shoved a roll into each of his pockets. Sticky and Damien joined him at the table and they gorged on the food. They then trailed off to wardrobe and changed into their rags. They giggled among themselves as they stood in comical poses.

Half an hour later the children had reassembled in STAGE C. Tommy asked them to form a single file and he walked down the line checking them out. Two make-up girls appeared and began dabbing the children's faces, legs and arms with large powderpuffs.

'Oh my God, they'll make us look like Boy George,' exclaimed Luke, as they reached him.

'Don't be silly. You'll be gorgeous. You won't recognise yourself,' smiled the redheaded girl as she removed Luke's hands from his face.

Luke's face becomes redder as the make-up was applied. 'I'll kill you if you breathe a word of this to anyone,' he said to the others through gritted teeth.

Sticky followed him back to their seats and

complained, 'I'm gonna make sure none of the lads ever finds out. I'd never live it down.'

Damien joined them and was equally critical. 'Bet they never put stuff like this on Harrison Ford or Tom Cruise.'

A loud roar from Tommy interrupted the lads' moaning. 'Quiet everybody and listen up.' As a hush fell over the children, he gave them further instructions. 'Right everybody, follow me onto the set and don't touch a thing.'

Quietly the children followed him across the roadway to Stage B. There they entered an amazing set. It was a rundown classroom of the mid-1850s, complete with furniture of the period. The set was lit by large arc lamps, stage crew were making some finishing touches and the cameraman was adjusting his camera. The children's eyes opened in amazement as they entered this wonder world. They had never seen the likes of it before. Stepping over cables, they moved to the centre of the set. Technicians busily moved all about them.

'Would you take a look at that,' exclaimed Luke, walking backwards.

'Will you all sit down at the desks,' instructed Tommy.

The children sat on long wooden benches at old-fashioned desks. Luke, Sticky and Damien sat together.

'I'd swear this is like where my granny went to school,' remarked Damien.

'Jeepers, I never thought I'd be going to school during the holliers,' said Sticky.

'Don't forget you'll be getting paid for it this time,' muttered Luke.

'I'd pay them any day to be able to opt off school,' commented Damien.

Tommy walked to the top of the class and clapped his hands. 'Quieten down everybody. Let's get organised.'

Then from a side entrance a number of people entered the set. There was a small man with a baseball cap and goatee beard. Behind him came a woman with a script. The next one to enter was a thin man with long grey hair and old-fashioned clothes. Then came the biggest surprise for the children. It was Todd Harper, the young film star. His hair was short and he wore ragged clothes like the other boys. A muscular, bald Black man, dressed in a dark suit accompanied him. He reminded Luke of a baddy in a James Bond film.

'Is that really him?' exclaimed Sticky.

'Shush, will you,' muttered Luke. 'Do you want to get us all turfed out?'

Damien strained his eyes to get a closer look at Todd. 'He's tiny. He seemed much bigger in *Captain Mungo*.'

'Will you give over. He's hardly shrunk,' mumbled Sticky.

'Say Todd, will you sit in here,' said the man in the baseball cap to the young star.

Todd slid into the seat in front of the three lads. He half turned towards them and smiled. Damien was about to speak but Luke gave him a kick on the shins. He muffled a cry.

'Good morning, children. My name's Matt Turner and I'm the director. In this scene Mr Mullen, the teacher, is giving Todd a tough time. You're all to look scared and nervous,' he explained as he signalled to the camera. 'OK, let's give it a try.'

Sticky recognised the actor playing the teacher. He put his hand over his mouth and whispered, 'That's your man from the telly . . . ah . . . you know.'

'Quiet please!' roared Tommy.

'Action!' called the director.

Mr Mullen turned from the window and slowly approached Todd. He towered over him with his hands on his hips. 'One more word out of you and I'll have you sleeping with the pigs,' he menaced.

'But, sir,' protested Todd in a fake Irish accent.

The teacher continued to bellow at the boy so fiercely that the children began to feel that it was for real and actually became terrified. Luke's face grew pale and he felt his legs shaking. The director gave the actors some additional instructions and they repeated the scene. And again. And yet again. When they were repeating the scene for the fourth time Sticky grew weary and began to yawn.

The director threw a wobbly and shouted at Sticky. 'You've just ruined the scene. If I want you to yawn I will tell you to yawn. Right?'

Sticky's face grew crimson. 'Yes, sir . . . I'm sorry . . . it was an accident. I didn't mean it.'

Luke glared at Sticky.

The scene was repeated several more times before it was to the director's satisfaction. Finally a tea break was called and all the children were relieved.

'You're a right header, nearly landing us in it,' snapped Luke as they queued at the tea counter.

'I couldn't help it if I had to yawn,' protested Sticky as he milked his tea. The cup overflowed and dribbled down his trousers.

'And I thought Breandie was bad! This teacher is a real head wrecker. He has poor Todd in bits. I feel sorry for him,' said Damien, still pale from the ordeal.

Luke chucked a piece of fruitcake at him as they sat at the table. 'You're a right eejit. Sure anyone knows it's not for real. It's only makey-up.'

'I know that, stupid.'

'Where did Todd get the corny Irish accent? I thought he was American,' said Sticky.

Luke shook his head. 'Isn't he supposed to be Irish in the film. It would be daft if he was talking with a Yankee accent.'

'Suppose so. I wonder is he only being paid thirty quid a day?' wondered Sticky.

Damien laughed. 'Are you out of your mind, or what? I'd say he's getting a hundred times that amount – easy.'

'Sure that's not fair. He's only doing the same thing as us,' said Sticky, doing some mental arithmetic.

Luke added, 'I'd say he's getting at least a million dollars for the film.'

The break was soon over and the boys were ordered back to the set. The same scene was shot with the camera at different angles. The three lads were becoming restless and bored. They almost cheered when an hour's break was called. Luke wanted to see where Todd Harper was going but the big Black man escorted him out a side door.

Luke, Damien and Sticky were on tippy-toes in the queue for lunch but could see no food.

'What's going on? What are we going to eat?' asked Luke.

'Probably yucky green vegetables. I hate them,' moaned Sticky.

Their questions were soon answered. Each of the children was handed a packed lunch. They sat at the table and opened the bags. They removed each item and set them out on the table in front of them. There was a ham roll, yoghurt, an apple, a Mars bar and a can of Coke for each.

'Hey, this isn't half bad,' said Luke cheering up.

Sticky held up his apple. 'Anyone want to do a swap? I don't fancy these. Maybe for a Mars bar?'

'You've got to be kidding,' laughed Damien. 'And anyway, apples are supposed to be good for you. Keep your teeth clean, and all.'

With no takers for his apple, Sticky was forced to eat it himself. Luke swivelled on his chair and looked around at the faces. 'I don't see Todd Harper. I wonder where he's got to?'

'He's probably tucking into steak and chicken and salmon. I'd say he lives a rare old life,' said Damien.

'It's well he can afford it. He's probably getting a bomb for this film too,' grumbled Luke.

'Yeah and we're only getting a mangy thirty quid. We should go on strike,' said Sticky, biting into his roll, the ham and salad squishing out on either side. Some salad dressing dripped onto his trousers.

'You're a messy sod, Sticky. You're ruining your clothes. Look at the state of them,' complained Damien.

'Sure they're only rags,' he laughed, wiping the food away. 'It will improve the look of them.'

'I'm fed up hanging around. Let's go out and play football,' said Luke, half-standing.

Sticky pulled him back onto the seat. 'What are you going to play with? Your brains?'

'Very smart,' jeered Luke. 'Let's see . . . eh. . . I have it! Give me over those empty bags.'

His two pals passed over their lunch bags. Luke rolled the three bags tightly together into the shape of a ball. 'How's that?' he asked, holding it over his head.

'Not bad,' replied Damien. 'Not bad at all.'

The three lads quickly finished their lunch and headed outdoors. They chose a quiet area at the rear of the studio beside two large trailers. Luke tossed the paper ball high in the air and Damien leapt to catch it. He threw it back to Luke who quickly returned it to him.

'Ah give us a go, lads,' called Sticky, reaching to grab the ball.

'Let's see how good you are,' teased Damien, throwing it higher.

Again Luke caught it and Sticky made a wild dart for him. 'No you don't,' yelled Luke quickly tossing it over his head.

Sticky began to sulk. 'That's not fair. Pass it to me.'

Just then the curtain on one of the trailer windows was drawn back. Todd's face appeared and he began to watch the boys playing. His head moved with interest from side to side as the paper ball was bounced about. The lads were unaware of him for a while.

Suddenly Sticky exclaimed, 'Hey Luke, look who's peeping out.'

Luke stopped in mid-action and glanced towards the trailer, saw Todd's smiling face and didn't know what to do. He smiled at the American star.

'Do you think we should ask him to play with us?' asked Luke of his pals.

'Are you mad or something?' exclaimed Damien. 'Didn't they say that we would be sent home straight away if we spoke to him.'

'Oh yeah, I nearly forgot that,' said Luke, disappointed.

'But only to play, that wouldn't hurt anyone,' said Sticky, smiling at the film star.

Luke shook his head. 'It's not worth the risk, lads. Wouldn't it be deadly to be able to tell every one that you played with Todd Harper but—'

'But then it would be the first and last time,' added Damien.

'Let's blow out of here then before we're in trouble,' said Luke, waving at Todd as they moved away. Todd waved after them and drew over the curtain.

'So this is where you are,' came Miss Foot's familiar voice. 'I might have guessed.'

The three boys stopped dead and stared at her. She didn't appear pleased.

'We were just—' Luke started to explain.

She pursed her lips and snapped. 'You shouldn't be here. This is for the stars. Get back on the set immediately.'

In the afternoon the boys remained in the classroom for further scenes. They grew more and more tired and bored as the day went on. They weren't sorry when they heard Tommy calling 'That's a wrap.' They knew that meant the end of the day's filming.

7. Cold Porridge

On leaving Ardmore Studios the three boys had mixed feelings. They were delighted to have spent their first day on a film set, especially to have worked with Todd Harper. Although they wanted to run down through the town telling everyone their news, they didn't dare. No way could they let their pals see their dire haircuts. They felt and looked like convicts. To make sure he wouldn't be spotted, Luke decided to take a roundabout way home. As he approached his estate he saw Mrs Mulligan, a nosy neighbour. He quickly hid behind a hedge until she had passed by. With his head down, he made a mad dash and kept running until he reached his back door.

'Oh Luke, you're back. I wasn't expecting you for ages,' his mother greeted him with surprise.

Luke plopped onto a chair in the kitchen and rested his head on the table.

'You must be joking. It's been the longest day of my life. I'm absolutely shattered.'

His mother rubbed his stubbly hair. 'You poor thing. Did you not enjoy it? Was it tough?'

Wearily he lifted his head. 'Ah no. Not really. It was deadly, Mam. You should have seen the state of the old school. The desks were ancient . . . and the lights . . . and the camera. It was brill. And you'll never guess who's in the film – Todd Harper! He looks better than he does in the films. You wouldn't believe it but they won't even let us talk to him,' he rattled off restlessly.

'Slow down, will you?' smiled his mother. 'Is that the same Todd Harper you said looked like a mammy's boy?'

'Ah but that was ages ago. He's OK now,' said Luke as he went to the sink to pour himself a glass of water.

'While you're there, you'd better rub off the rest of that make-up,' chuckled his mother. 'It goes well with the new hair-do!'

Luke quickly glanced in the mirror. 'Oh no, I thought I'd got rid of all that greasy stuff. It's gross,' he said as he scrubbed at the make-up with a tea towel.

There was a ring on the hall door. 'That's probably for you,' said Mrs Carroll nodding towards the door.

'No, you get it. If it's anyone for me I'm not in!' said Luke appearing uncomfortable.

This surprised his mother. 'That's most unlike you. Are you sick or something? You're never off the road.'

His face reddened again. 'Not with my hair like this. Are you joking? I'd die if anyone saw me.'

His mother burst out laughing. 'Now I've heard it all. Does that mean you won't be going down to the seafront or up to your den until your hair grows back?'

Luke was annoyed. 'I don't know. I'll see. Just tell them I'm not in.'

Mrs Carroll was still chuckling when she went to answer the hall door. Luke put his ear to the kitchen door and listened while his mother spoke to his pals. She returned to the kitchen a few moments later and smiled.

'I think I have the answer to your problem. Why don't you wear a woolly hat or a baseball cap? Nobody would be any the wiser.'

This seemed like a good idea to Luke. 'That could work. Sure I wear a baseball cap most of the summer anyway.'

'Where's that cap your Auntie Dee sent you for your

birthday last year? I think I saw it at the bottom of your wardrobe recently.'

'Deadly! And I thought I was going to have to stay indoors for weeks or else go out and get slagged,' said Luke looking a lot happier.

'You could even wear it in bed in case you meet anyone in your dreams,' laughed his mum.

'Very funny!' Luke ran upstairs, grabbed his baseball cap and was off out the door after his pals.

'Are you going to the den?' called Barbara.

'Yeah,' replied her brother, as he carried Castro outside.

'Wait for me,' she cried.

Within minutes Barbara and the three boys were on their bikes and cycling up the Greystones road. They turned right at Windgates and travelled along a country road by the walls of Killruddery Estate. Stopping at a section of the wall where the bricks had collapsed, they carried their bikes through the gap and across the field to the wood where their den was located. It was situated in an old lodge at the base of the Little Sugarloaf. Lord Meath had generously given them the disused empty building as a reward for foiling a robbery in his house the previous summer.

The children abandoned their bikes in the high grass outside the lodge. Luke collected the key from under a rock. Then he fumbled about with the lock without having any success in opening the door.

'Give it to me,' demanded Barbara, pushing Luke aside. She managed to open the door on the first attempt.

'Thinks she knows everything,' muttered Damien.

'Ugh, the smell!' cried Barbara, as they entered the building. 'It's worse than your room!'

'Don't start,' snapped Luke. 'Do you want us to bring up the hoover and polish?'

Barbara shook her head as she stepped over a broken pallet. 'It mightn't be a bad idea at that.'

'And what about that fresh air stuff Mam's always spraying?' added Luke.

Sticky became ratty. 'Will you pair knock it off. Anyone would swear it was a palace. It's only a den. I get enough stick at home about cleaning up.'

The children sat around in a semi-circle. The boys squatted on the floor while Barbara sat on the only chair. Castro sat on Luke's knee.

'I've a massive idea,' said Damien thoughtfully.

They all waited for him to elaborate but he said nothing.

'Are we supposed to guess what this massive idea is?' snapped Luke.

'Oh yeah,' nodded Damien. 'Wouldn't it be great if we got posters from some of Todd's films.'

'That's a deadly idea and we could cover all the cracks in the walls with them,' said Sticky excitedly.

'Typical,' said Barbara sarcastically. 'It'll save you lazy sods from having to paint the walls.'

'Would you ever give it a rest,' moaned Luke.

The thought of having to get up at six o'clock the following morning had Luke in bed at nine o'clock. Even with the curtains drawn, his room was still bright, so he hung towels over the curtain rails to keep the sun out. From pure exhaustion he was asleep in ten minutes.

The next morning at the studio Luke, Damien and

Sticky, familiar with the routine, quickly changed into their ragged clothes. They hurried to STAGE C for their tea and rolls.

Twenty minutes later Tommy escorted them to another set. This was a long dimly-lit dining room. Two narrow tables ran the length of the room with benches on either side. At the top of the room there was a big solid table with several enormous pots. The director, Todd Harper and some other actors were standing at the top of the room. Tommy indicated to the young extras to sit at the long tables. Luke, Sticky and Damien sat side by side. A bowl and wooden spoon was placed in front of each of them.

Damien rubbed his hands with glee. 'This is great. We're going to get fed as well.'

'Hope it's Weetabix. They're my favourite,' said Sticky, examining the bowl.

'You should be so lucky,' commented Luke.

Their questions were soon answered when a large man with a sweat-stained shirt and dirty trousers moved from boy to boy dropping a huge dollop of cold porridge into their bowls.

'Yuck, look at the state of that,' moaned Luke.

Sticky lifted up the bowl to smell it. 'It smells like—'

Damien cut across him. 'I hate porridge more than anything else. It makes me puke just to look at it.'

Tommy shouted commands over the din of the children. 'Listen up everybody. When you hear the word 'ACTION' I want you to start eating the porridge . . . really gobble it up . . . pretend you're starving. Understood? Are there any questions?'

'I'd love to ask him if he'd eat this stuff himself,' muttered Sticky.

Damien grew pale. 'I'll go home before I eat a speck.'

'Hey we could always turn our spoons upside down and pretend we're eating,' suggested Luke.

'That's an idea. Worth a try,' Damien sounded hopeful.

The lads had to wait about fifteen minutes until they heard the word 'ACTION' and then, heads lowered, spoons upside down, they pretended to eat the cold porridge. In the scene Todd Harper refused to eat the cold food and a row developed with one of the priests from the orphanage. The scene was repeated over and over and the bowls were topped up with fresh porridge. On realising this Luke and his two pals began to drop handfuls of porridge onto the floor so that no one would notice they were not eating. During the next take, a boy close to them puked up over the table. He was taken away by the studio nurse while the mess was cleaned up.

When they broke for lunch, Luke hurried outside and waited close to Todd's trailer. Soon Todd and his minder appeared. Luke pretended to be resting against the wall. Todd smiled and winked at Luke as he entered his trailer. Luke was about to speak but bit his tongue and smiled back. He was afraid he would be sent home if he said anything. He was determined to find a way of talking to the young American.

Luke joined Sticky and Damien who were enjoying their packed lunches and sunning themselves on a green patch beside the studio.

'You're looking for trouble, you know that, don't you?' said Damien, tucking into his Mars bar.

'And you needn't bother walking us two into it as well. If you want to be sent packing, you can do it on your own,' warned Sticky.

'You're all scaredy cats. Afraid to chance anything. Real nancy boys. I don't know why I bother with you,' grumbled Luke.

Luke didn't have to wait long to make contact with Todd. After lunch the boys sat back at the tables facing their bowls of porridge. The director, Todd and his minder came back onto the set. As Todd passed by, he dropped his script on the floor. Luke quickly bent down to pick it up. He handed it to Todd who grinned and said 'Thanks'.

Luke blushed and he smiled. Todd leaned forward and slipped a folded piece of paper into Luke's hand. Then he moved on to the top of the class.

Slowly Luke opened the palm of his hand and gradually unfolded the piece of paper. It read, 'Hi, would you get your telephone number to me? Todd.'

Sticky leaned over to see what he was reading. 'What's that?'

'Shush,' whispered Luke, discreetly holding the piece of paper towards him.

Sticky was astonished. 'What! He wants your phone number. What for?'

'Give over,' whispered Luke. 'Do you want someone to hear and get us chucked out?'

'What is he going to do with your number?' wondered Damien,

'Ring me, thicko!' Luke replied in a fierce whisper.

'Are you going to give it to him?' enquired Sticky.

'Of course, wouldn't you? It's not every day a film star asks you for your telephone number,' answered Luke, tearing a piece off his lunch bag which was in his pocket.

He borrowed a pen from an assistant director and wrote his name and telephone number on the paper when

63

he thought nobody was looking. He waited all afternoon hoping for an opportunity to get near Todd. His chance came when Tommy called for a tea break. Luke headed straight for Todd and, brushing against him, he shoved the piece of paper into his hand. Todd winked at him.

That night as Luke was watching MTV he heard the phone ringing. He was too tired to answer it. He heard his mother speaking on the phone and then she called to him.

'Luke, it's for you.'

'OK,' he answered wearily, climbing off the couch. 'Yeah?' he grumbled into the mouthpiece.

'Luke . . . this is Todd Harper,' came the voice.

'Ah come off it Sticky. I'm not in humour for jokes. I'm knackered. I'm not amused.'

'I'm serious,' laughed Todd. 'I asked you for your number today on the set.'

Luke almost dropped the phone with the shock. 'It's . . . It's really you . . . I'm not supposed to talk to you.'

Todd wasn't bothered. 'Don't worry, I won't tell anyone. Will you?'

'No way. Do you think I'm mad?' he replied. 'Well, it must be deadly for you. Being in the films. I saw every one of your movies. I think you're great.'

'Thanks, Luke,' said Todd. 'It's not bad, but I miss my mom and dad and my friends. I wish I could be like you and your buddies, playing football and having a good time.'

'But surely you can do what you like?' asked Luke.

Todd sighed. 'You gotta be kidding. I have a minder with me all the time. I don't get to play with other kids. They're afraid I could get hurt.'

'That's awful,' replied Luke, in disbelief. 'Can you

never get out to play a match with some of your friends or even go to the cinema?'

Todd gave a loud laugh. 'I wish I could. Everywhere I go I need to have adults with me. That's why I was hoping I might be able to get together with you guys.'

'With us?' exclaimed Luke. 'You mean to play a match, or hang around?'

'Something like that. Got any ideas?' asked Todd.

'I can't think of anything off the top of my head. How would you get away?' asked Luke.

Todd muttered, 'Um . . . I'm staying in the Knockcrone Hotel in Enniskerry . . . do you know it?'

'Oh boy, that's really posh. It must cost an arm and a leg to stay there,' said Luke enviously.

'I'm sure it does. But I don't have to pay for it myself,' explained Todd.

'You lucky sod,' exclaimed Luke. 'But are you serious about wanting to hang around with us?'

'Sure am. I'd love to,' said Todd, lowering his voice. 'I'll have to go – someone's coming. Good luck. Talk to you soon.'

'Thanks a lot . . . Todd,' said Luke, hanging up the receiver. He charged into the kitchen and yelled, 'That was Todd Harper, ringing me up.'

His mother shook her head. 'Is this another of your tall tales, Luke? You're always coming up with them.'

'Honest, cross my heart and hope to die. Sure you even spoke to him yourself,' said Luke, leaping about.

His mother was thoughtful. 'Hmmm . . . he did have an American accent all right. What did he want with you? I thought you were forbidden to speak to him?'

'We are, but he wanted to talk to me,' he boasted.

'He wants to try to get together . . . he said—'

His mother cut across him with a warning. 'You be careful now, Luke. They do things differently in America. Don't get yourself into trouble.'

'I won't.'

8. In the Bog

Monday was always the worst day of the week. Luke hated Mondays. The thought of another week at school was enough to make him feel sick. In the past he thought up every excuse in the book to avoid getting out of bed and going to school on Monday mornings. His parents had fallen for none of his excuses or tall stories and he was normally hauled out of bed protesting and sent to school regardless.

This Monday was different. Luke was awake long before his father called him. He was out of bed, dressed and washed and downstairs in the kitchen just after six o'clock. Mr Carroll whispered to his wife, 'I hope this continues when he's back at school.'

If Luke, Sticky and Damien thought that the scenes in the dining room with the cold porridge were tough and boring they had a lot worse in store for them today.

Arriving at the studio they went through the usual routine of changing into their costumes and eating their breakfast of tea and rolls. They played push penny on the table while they waited for instructions from Tommy.

'Right everybody. Outside and onto the bus,' ordered Tommy.

'This sounds more interesting,' said Luke as the boys immediately made for the door and trundled onto the bus outside. There was an air of excitement among the children.

'Where are they taking us? Are we not going to be in the film today?' asked Sticky, still chewing on a roll.

Damien looked puzzled. 'Maybe they're bringing us home again.'

'Don't be daft,' said Luke, 'sure all our clothes are here. They must be filming somewhere else today.'

'Maybe we're going on location,' said Sticky. 'That's what they call it when you go off somewhere else to film.'

'You mean like to Hollywood?' enquired Damien hopefully.

'Hollywood, County Wicklow,' laughed Luke.

The boys were still speculating as the bus pulled out of the studio and onto the Enniskerry Road. They passed through the village of Enniskerry and on up the steep hill towards Glencree.

As they drove by a high hedge Damien yelled out, 'Hey look. That's my Uncle Peter's farm – can we call in?'

'Try asking the driver,' joked Luke.

'Are you serious, do you think he'll stop?' asked Damien, falling for the joke.

'Would you ever knock it off. We're not on a school tour, we're working men now,' said Sticky.

The bus spluttered up the hill behind the Glencree Reconciliation Centre. Soon they were looking down into Glencree Valley with magnificent views of the Sugarloaf and Bray Head and the Irish Sea in the distance.

'Look at all those trucks and limos,' shouted Sticky, pointing to a line of vehicles parked at the side of the bog.

'They must all have broken down, there's nothing up here to visit but turf and sheep,' said Damien.

Luke threw his eyes to heaven. 'You eejit, they're all part of the film crew.'

'But isn't this film supposed to be set in the olden days, surely they hadn't got those kind of cars then,' said Sticky.

The bus parked on the grass verge beside a mobile

generator. Tommy appeared at the door and clapped his hands. 'Chop, chop! Everybody out! Make it snappy. We've got a lot of work to do.'

'Is he mad, sure we'll catch our death of cold up here,' moaned Sticky, as they filed off the bus.

The group of boys hobbled along the road in their bare feet. Tommy led them past the trucks and limos to where the camera and arc lamps had been erected. Todd Harper and the other actors stood at the edge of the bog getting their instructions. Four soldiers dressed as redcoats, carrying muskets, sat on the rear flap of the props truck. They looked funny in their splendid uniforms, drinking coffee out of plastic cups.

'Good morning, lads.' The director was talking to them. 'All in good form, I trust? No hangovers? I hope you're in the mood for action, because we've got plenty lined up for you today.'

He's very cheerful for a Monday morning, Luke thought to himself. This is more like my kind of day, anything is better than sitting around looking into a bowl of porridge.

The director waved his arms about as he explained, 'In this scene you will be walking two by two along the track. The redcoats will appear over the hill and get into a firing position. This is the signal for you to scatter and run for cover, looking scared. When the soldiers open fire, throw yourselves to the ground, and stay down no matter what you hear. Remember: No looking at the camera!

Luke's face lit up. 'This is more like it. Real guns and shooting.'

Damien wasn't so sure, 'But . . . but they might kill us by accident. I'm not—'

69

'Don't be such a scaredy cat. They're not real bullets,' said Luke, patting him on the back.

'It's all right for you,' whinged Damien. 'You haven't got a nerve in your body.'

Their voices were drowned out by Tommy shouting orders through a megaphone. 'Into twos everybody and start walking up the trail. When you reach that big rock on the right, stop and wait.'

The children did as they were instructed and made their way carefully over the stony surface. They waited at the rock and Todd and other actors were placed in positions among them. The make-up people moved from one to the other applying make-up. On the shout of 'ACTION' they walked on until the redcoats appeared over the hill.

'Scatter, scatter,' yelled Luke, turning abruptly and tearing back down the track.

Somebody stood on Damien's toe and he yelped in pain as he grabbed his foot. A number of boys crashed into him and pushed him face down in the bog. He sank slowly into the brownish-black bog water. The water and mud seeped into his mouth. He spat it out.

Sticky dived behind a furze bush and ducked his head as the shots rang out.

'CUT!' roared the director. 'Well done, everybody. That was great. We'll try it one more time.'

Luke stood up and brushed himself down. This is terrific, he thought. He was ready to do it again and again. Most of the other lads didn't agree with him and were fairly shaken, especially Damien. Slowly he pushed himself up onto his knees; he was covered in mucky bog water. He wiped his face with the back of his hand.

Gradually he stood upright, his legs wobbling. The dirty water trickled down his back, legs and arms.

Luke burst out laughing. 'Would you take a look at him. He's a real bog man now.'

The make-up girl came to Damien and began wiping him with a towel. She cleaned off the dirt with cotton wool. 'You'll be grand now,' she smiled.

Sticky stuck out his tongue and jeered. 'You'd need more than that to make him a pretty sight.'

'Stop hanging around, everybody. Into place again. There's work to be done,' snapped Tommy.

'This is deadly,' cheered Luke, enjoying every moment of it. 'I wonder will they let us pelt stones at the soldiers? Should I mention it to them?'

'Are you out of your mind? You'll get us all sent home,' said Sticky, cleaning mud from his ear.

Everybody returned to their first positions and prepared to repeat the scene. Damien stood between Luke and Sticky and gave a big sigh.

Luke leaned over and whispered into Damien's ear, 'Watch for the bullets. I hear they'll be firing live rounds this time.'

Damien sniffled, 'Anymore of this and I'm going home.'

'I'd hate to see you in a real battle,' mocked Sticky. 'You'd probably be crying for your mammy.'

'Ha, ha, very funny,' muttered Damien, still squeezing water out of his costume.

While they were still arguing, the director shouted 'ACTION'. They walked up the track again until the redcoats appeared. As the shots rang out the boys turned and ran.

This time Luke tripped and rolled off the track into the bog. He landed on his back and the slimy bog water surged in around him. He sat upright before the water could cover his face. He felt extremely uncomfortable and was relieved when the director called 'CUT'.

Damien stood, hands on hips, roaring laughing and pointing at him. 'Now who looks a right eejit? Are you playing with the tadpoles?'

Todd Harper passed by and smiled down at Luke. 'Hi, Luke, why don't you try taking a bath in clean water?'

Luke's face reddened as he climbed out of the bog. The make-up girls stifled a smile as they approached him with a towel. They began drying his hair.

'See – it can happen to anyone,' laughed the girl. ' Are you OK?'

'Yeah,' Luke grunted, with only his pride hurt.

The lads continued mocking him.

'Did you like the taste of it?' teased Damien.

'They should have left it on you, you looked like the Mummy's brother,' cackled Sticky.

Luke's temper was beginning to boil. 'If you don't belt up, you'll be sorry,' he muttered darkly, although he knew he deserved some ribbing for laughing at Damien.

'There you are, as good as new, ready for another round,' said the make-up girl.

'Come on Luke, it's great gas. Cheer up. Sure beats going to school any day,' said Sticky.

'Suppose so,' grunted Luke. He turned to see everybody heading down the road. 'Where are they off to?'

'Maybe to that bus,' said Damien pointing towards a very old bus which was parked a short distance away.

The lads were surprised to find that the bus had tables and chairs inside arranged like a little restaurant. It had been converted specially for use on occasions like this. They were handed two slices of cake and a cup of coffee each as they boarded.

'Boy, this is something else,' said Damien as he sipped his coffee.

'I wonder will we get a chance to use any of the guns and shoot back at the soldiers,' said Sticky hopefully.

'Not likely, they wouldn't let us loose with guns,' stated Luke.

'And I wouldn't trust us either,' laughed Sticky.

'I was just thinking . . . do you know who is the spittin' image of Todd Harper?' said Damien thoughtfully.

'No. Who?' answered Luke, impatiently.

'David Nolan! Take a good look at him during the next scene. You'll see I'm right,' explained Damien.

Sticky bit his lip as he thought. 'Come to think of it you could be right. His hair is the same colour, and he has the same kind of teeth.'

Luke's face brightened. 'That gives me an idea. It could be just what we're looking for.'

Sticky was puzzled. 'What's that got to do with anything?'

'Todd would like to get together with us. Now if we could get David Nolan to help out—' said Luke gleefully as a plot was beginning to form in his head.

'David Nolan . . .' began Damien. 'He's a right nerd. Thinks he knows everything. God's gift to people!'

'And always trying to get into our gang,' scoffed Sticky. 'There's no way we're letting him in, and that's final.'

'He's not a bad footballer, though,' added Damien.

'Give over, lads, I'm trying to think,' said Luke thoughtfully.

Before he could finish his planning, Tommy had called them back onto the bog to repeat the scene.

9. Luke's Plan

When they finished filming for the day Luke sprinted home. His mother ran a bath for him and he soaked in it for over half an hour. Noticing that there was a salad for tea Luke said that he wasn't hungry. Instead he grabbed a voucher off the hallstand and went and got himself a Big Mac and Coke in McDonalds.

Luke returned for his BMX and cycled up to Ardmore Park. He spotted David Nolan and his sister, Andrea, flying a kite on the green.

'Hiya David, how's it going?' shouted Luke, as he ran his bike onto the grass.

David half turned. 'Oh Luke, what are you doing up here?'

Luke sprang off his bike and walked towards David. 'Nothing special. Just thought I might see you.'

'Hey David, look out. Are you playing or not?' cried Andrea.

David passed her the string of the kite. 'Here . . . I'm not playing any more. I want to talk to Luke.'

'Trust you, you're always the same. Can never stay at anything,' snapped his sister as she walked away in a sulk.

'I haven't seen you in ages. How's the work on the film going?' asked David, walking over to sit on a low garden wall.

Luke sat beside him. 'Not bad . . . has boring bits but beats school any day.'

'Did you see Todd Harper?'

Luke lifted his head and said boastfully, 'I see him every day and I've even spoken to him. He's really cool!'

'I love his films,' exclaimed David.

'Yeah, he's all right but we're not allowed to talk to him,' said Luke.

David was really impressed by what he was hearing. 'I'd give anything to meet him.'

Luke ran his tongue over his lower teeth and sat thinking for a minute. 'Do you still want to join our gang?'

David nodded enthusiastically. 'Oh yeah, definitely.'

'Well, everyone who joins has to do a challenge.'

David was growing more eager by the second. 'I'll do anything to get in. Just name it.'

Luke began making up the plan as he spoke. 'It would involve Todd Harper. You might have to stand in for him so that he could sneak out of his hotel. Are you on for it?'

David was confused. 'But wouldn't everybody know I wasn't him. I don't look a bit like him. I can't even speak with an American accent.'

'None of that matters. Just tell me are you game to give it a try or not, if I get anything organised?'

'Sure, you can rely on me.'

'Great, that's settled,' said Luke, hopping off the wall. 'I'll give you a shout when it's on.'

'I can't wait,' said David, waving at Luke.

Luke cycled home feeling happy with himself. Part one of his plan was in place. He was sure that getting David to agree was the most difficult part. The next thing he had to do was talk to Todd and fill him in.

The following morning Luke scribbled out a note and waited for an opportunity to pass it to Todd. Much to everybody's discomfort they were filming up on the bog again. It was a cooler day and a heavy mist capped the mountain top.

The boys stayed in the bus as long as they could and only came onto the bog when the crew was ready for filming. As Luke passed by Todd he slipped the note into his hand. During the tea break Todd dropped a piece of paper as he neared Luke. It read 'Luke, if you come and stand beside my trailer window at lunchtime I will try and talk to you. Todd.'

Luke felt excited and nervous as he waited for the lunch break. He collected his packed lunch and discreetly slipped away. Checking that nobody was watching, he squatted on the ground beneath one of the windows of Todd's trailer. He began eating his ham roll. From time to time he threw a glance over his shoulder at the window but there was nobody there. After a few minutes he heard a gentle tap on the window. He looked up to see Todd signalling to him. Todd opened out the window a fraction.

'Hi Luke, great to see you,' said Todd.

Luke tried to talk with his mouth full. 'I think I have something figured out. If it works you'll be able to get out for the night.'

Todd was delighted with the news. 'What's the plan?'

Luke took a swig out of his can of Coke before talking. 'Well, there's this guy, David Nolan. He's a real . . . ah nothing. You'd want to see him. He wants to join our gang and I've got him to help us. He looks a bit like you. I . . . I . . . eh . . . don't mean you look like—' he said, becoming embarrassed.

Todd began laughing. 'I know what you mean. Go on, keep talking.'

With his cheeks red, Luke continued. 'Well I thought we might be able to do a switch. If there was some way we could sneak him into your hotel, then you could sneak out.'

'Hey, I like the sound of that,' began Todd. 'Emm . . . let's see. Would you be able to find the Knockcrone Hotel, where I'm staying?'

Luke chewed his lip thoughtfully. 'Yeah, I think so. It wouldn't be up a big hill at the side of a wood?'

Todd clicked his fingers. 'That's the one. What if you and your pals come along at seven o'clock tonight? I'm in a corner room on the second floor at the right-hand side of the hotel. I'll signal down to you.'

Luke was growing more and more excited. 'You'll definitely come out with us?' he asked.

Todd gave a broad grin. 'Try stopping me.' He paused and glanced over his shoulder. 'I think someone's coming. You'd better go.'

'Be seeing you then,' said Luke, standing up.

Todd closed the window and Luke could hear the young actor talking to someone. Luke hurried off to update Sticky and Damien. They were sitting on the bus finishing off their lunches.

'Where did you get to?' queried Damien. 'We were looking for you everywhere.'

'I thought you'd fallen into the bog again,' sniggered Sticky.

Luke held a finger to his lips. 'Shush will you, I don't want anyone to hear.'

The boys lowered their heads over the table as Luke sat opposite them. 'Everything's on for tonight, lads. I want you to meet at my house at six o'clock. I'll bring David Nolan if—'

Sticky cut in sharply. 'You're not bringing him surely?'

Luke frowned. 'Don't start, Sticky, I'm warning you.

If Nolan doesn't come the plan is totally washed up. Do you get that? Or do you want me to scrap the whole idea?'

'OK, OK, keep your hair on. I was only saying,' said Sticky holding up his hand in a gesture of peace.

'And tell us, is Todd going to be able to talk to us?' asked Damien.

Luke nodded. 'If none of you muck it up.'

'You can count on me. I'm a sound man,' Sticky assured him.

The afternoon didn't go fast enough for the boys. They were only sorry they were not allowed to wear their watches so that they could check the time. Excitement was mounting in each of them and they were looking forward to their big adventure. When Tommy call 'WRAP' for the day they made a sprint for the bus and were soon on their way to Ardmore. Back at the studio they hurried to the wardrobe section and tore off their rags.

Luke made the journey to his house in record time. He dug out his piggybank from under his bed and put its contents into the pocket of his jeans. He gulped down his tea and called to his mother as he raced out, 'I'll be late in.' Before she could question him, he had disappeared.

Luke kept his finger on the doorbell at David Nolan's house until David appeared at the door. 'We're off now. Are you ready?' demanded Luke.

'Well I was going to—' began David.

Luke gritted his teeth and snapped. 'What are you playing at? If you don't come now, that's it! It's kaput. The deal's off for good. Now, are you coming or not?'

David sighed and shrugged. 'OK then.'

'You'll need your bike,' instructed Luke.

Immediately David disappeared inside and returned

minutes later round the gable end of the house wheeling his BMX. The boys leapt onto their bikes and raced across the green.

By the time they reached Luke's house, Sticky and Damien were waiting there with their bikes. Luke checked his watch and decided it was time to leave. They travelled on the flyover across the N11 Motorway and up the narrow Enniskerry Road. On the steepest sections of the road they stood on the pedals to give themselves maximum speed. On reaching the picturesque village of Enniskerry, they stopped under the clock tower.

'Where to now?' asked Damien, resting his foot against the water trough.

'I think it's about two miles this way,' said Luke indicating the sharp uphill road ahead of them.

Damien pulled a face when he saw the hill. 'Cycle up there? Do you think I'm Stephen Roche?'

Luke didn't reply, but took off at speed up the hill. The others followed with Damien trailing behind. When they reached the brow of the hill, they were able to freewheel all the way down to the gates of the Knockcrone Hotel. Luke skidded to a halt on the gravel beside one of the two large gateposts topped with ornamental eagles.

'What now?' enquired Sticky.

'We'll have to sneak around the back without being seen. If we're spotted we'll be chucked out and it will wreck everything. Be on the alert,' said Luke, peeping around the pillar.

'Is it OK?' asked David, looking anxious.

'Come on quick. The coast is clear. Remember, not a peep out of anyone,' said Luke, urgently waving them on.

The boys ran into the trees which ran parallel with the

driveway, wheeling their bikes beside them. They continued through the undergrowth for a few minutes until they came to a clearing. In front of them there was a landscaped lawn which ran all the way to the impressive Victorian hotel. There were spires on either end of the building and lots of carved heads of ancient gods. Luke waited until the others caught up with him.

'Phew! It's a castle!' exclaimed David.

'Looks creepy to me,' said Damien.

'Probably haunted,' Luke decided.

'I'd say it costs an arm and a leg to stay there,' added Damien.

Sticky was also impressed. 'You'd have to win the Lotto to be able to afford chicken and chips there.'

David turned to him. 'You wouldn't get chicken and chips in this posh hotel. More like caviar and lobster.'

'Would you listen to him. What would you know about it?' snapped Sticky.

'Will you all give over talking about food. You're making me hungry,' whispered Luke crossly. 'The first thing we've got to do is to find out which room Todd is in. He said it's on the right-hand corner of the second floor.'

'What about the bikes? What will we do with them?' asked Sticky.

'You stay here and keep an eye on them until we get back,' instructed Luke.

'Why me?' moaned Sticky.

Luke gave him a little shove. 'You shouldn't have asked, should you?'

He moved forward, urging the others into action. 'Quick, before anyone comes.'

Running across the clearing, they stopped beside the

wall of the hotel. The window on the corner of the second floor opened slowly and Todd's head appeared over the window ledge.

'Are you coming up?' he called down.

'He's on his way,' replied Luke, giving David a push.

David grabbed onto the ivy and drew himself up. He secured a grip for his foot and Luke gave him a leg up to get him on his way. 'Give over, I'll manage on my own,' exclaimed David.

Luke drew back and gave a deep sigh as he watched David's slow progress up the ivy-clad wall. Silently they stood watching him.

Suddenly there was the sound of a door opening at the rear of the hotel. They all froze. Luke took cover behind a bush. Damien flattened against the wall of the hotel and moved cautiously to where he could peep around the corner. He saw a kitchen porter putting empty bottles into a container. David clung quietly to the ivy, his face very white. His heart was pounding and his right leg was twitching. He felt cold sweat running down the back of his tee shirt. Tension mounted when the porter lit up a cigarette. If he decided to stroll to the corner they would be caught. However, luck was on their side when a voice from the kitchen called the porter back to his work.

With the back of his hand Luke wiped sweat from his forehead.

'Go on – make it snappy before anyone else comes,' he whispered to David as loudly as he dared.

David inched his way up, a little faster this time. He tightly gripped the stems of the ivy as Todd encouraged him from the window ledge. 'Great, keep going. You're nearly there.'

David turned to look down. Realising how far he was from the ground he panicked and froze where he was, unable to move.

'Don't look down, you fool,' whispered Sticky.

'Give me your hand,' said Todd, reaching down to David.

'I . . . I can't . . . I'm scared . . . I'll fall if I let go,' stuttered David.

Todd smiled at him. 'It's simple. Just reach up to me. It's not as bad as it looks.'

David stretched his hand and strained every muscle in his body until Todd could catch hold of him. The American boy gripped David's hand tightly and eased him up, little by little.

'That's cool. Nearly there. Just push with your feet.'

Within minutes David was clambering over the windowsill into the room, landing with a bump on the floor. He was shaking and almost breathless. Todd patted him on the back and said, 'Good man, you did great,' as he helped him to his feet.

'What do you want me to do now?' asked David brushing down his clothes and hair with his hands.

'Right, I have it figured out. You hop into my bed and keep your face turned away from the door,' explained Todd, as he led David across the biggest bedroom the boy had ever seen.

'OK, but what will I do if anyone comes in?' asked David, still uneasy with the plan.

Todd nodded and said,. 'I've told them I was tired and was going to bed early. But just to be sure, I have a tape. Listen!' He pressed the 'play' button on a small tape recorder and David heard Todd's voice speaking in a sleepy tone, 'I'm tired . . . leave me alone . . . I'll see you in the morning.'

'Hey, that's brilliant,' said David. 'OK. I'll give it a try.'

'I've left you some cookies and Hershey Bars and a bottle of Coke,' Todd said kindly. 'I hope you like them.'

'Thanks a lot,' said David.

'See you later, buddy,' smiled Todd, as he put on his baseball cap before climbing out the window. He quickly scrambled down the ivy without pausing.

Luke and Damien looked at him in amazement.

'You were like Spiderman,' Luke whispered when the boy was down. 'How did you do that so fast?'

Todd laughed. 'It's easy. I've watched so many stunt guys in my movies, I study them. It's not so difficult.'

'I wish I could do that,' said Damien, full of admiration.

'Listen, we'd better get the skids on. It's getting late,' said Luke, as he urged them to sprint across the lawn. Todd and Damien took off after him.

'I know Luke here,' said Todd when they reached the bikes, 'but what are your names?'

Sticky and Damien introduced themselves.

'What happens now?' enquired Todd.

'We're going to cycle into Bray,' explained Luke, as he picked up David's bike. 'You can take this one,' he offered the bike to Todd.

'Thanks, Luke. I haven't been on one of these for ages,' said Todd, inspecting the bike.

'I bet you have a super-duper bike at home,' said Sticky, climbing onto his own bike.

Todd smiled as he sat on the saddle. 'Believe it or not, I don't have one of my own. But don't worry, I'll be fine.'

84

'Everybody set?' shouted Luke. 'Away we go.' He cycled out through the hotel gates, with the other boys following close behind.

10. The Great Adventure

Luke led the bunch freewheeling down the hill to Enniskerry; Todd tore past them, giving a loud roar.

'He's OK – isn't he? He's just like us, he's normal,' said Sticky breathlessly.

Luke slowed up to let Sticky catch up with him. 'What did you expect? That he'd be wearing a halo? Just because he's a big star doesn't mean he's not normal. Don't go rubbing him up the wrong way, do you hear?'

'What do you take me for?' muttered Sticky.

Luke didn't answer and took off after Todd. They cycled in single file along the narrow road and passed along the banks of the Dargle River. When a loud blast sounded from the horn of a truck coming up behind them, they moved carefully onto the footpath.

As they cycled down Herbert Road, Todd let out a yell. 'Hey, there's the studio. If they could see me now.'

'Do you want to pay them a visit?' joked Luke.

'No way! I'd be handcuffed to my minder for good,' laughed the young American, pulling his baseball cap sideways to conceal his face.

The boys turned onto Killarney Road, ignoring the red light at the Town Hall. They zigzagged between the traffic in the Main Street and whizzed down the Quinsboro Road past the Royal Cinema where there was a queue for Todd's latest film. They skidded to a halt at the level crossing and waited at the barrier while the DART arrived from Dublin.

'Hey, that's a cool train, a bit like the BART,' said Todd, leaning over the barrier to watch it passing.

'No, you eejit, it's called the Dart,' said Sticky, amused.

Todd laughed loudly. 'I didn't mean the one in Bray, I meant the train in Frisco.'

Sticky pulled a face. 'Frisco . . . Frisco . . . what's this Frisco, is it some sort of washing-up liquid?'

Luke clipped Sticky across the head. 'He means San Francisco in America. Do you know nothing?'

'Oh that Frisco! Were you ever in San Francisco, Todd?' asked Sticky.

Todd shouted over his shoulder as the barrier lifted and they cycled towards the seafront. 'Sure thing, I live there.'

'Boy, you lucky sod. I'd give anything to go there,' said Damien, enviously. 'The hills . . . and cable cars . . . earthquakes.'

'It's OK, but I haven't seen any earthquakes yet. Maybe some day I will,' replied Todd as they cycled on.

'Wasn't one of the James Bond films made on the Golden Gate Bridge?' asked Luke.

'Yeah sure, I remember that one. What was it called?' asked Todd.

Sticky cycled up beside Todd. 'Is the snow really six feet deep there?'

Todd threw back his head and laughed. 'Snow . . . what snow? We never get snow . . . rain and fog yes, but no snow. You have to go to Chicago or New York to get snow.'

'Must be deadly, all the same, in America. When I get older it's one of the first places I want to go to,' said Luke, as he raced ahead along Strand Road.

'Hey, where are we headed?' called Todd.

'You'll find out soon enough,' Luke shouted back.

The boys cycled to the end of the seafront. Luke was first to hop off his bike. The others followed suit. They took the chains which were wrapped around the crossbars and locked the bikes together to a No Parking sign.

'Are they safe here?' asked Todd.

'Of course! Who'd dare to nick them? They know better,' said Damien with bravado.

Luke led them into Dawsons Amusements. It was a bustle of activity and excitement with the combined noise of machinery, music and screaming children.

Todd was astonished and his eyes opened wide. He glanced from the waltzer to the dodgems to the pinball machines.

'What do you think of it?' asked Luke, shouting to be heard.

'It's fantastic . . . really amazing. I was never in a place like this before,' Todd replied.

Damien was surprised. 'You weren't? But you have Disneyland and all those amazing places in America.'

'I know. I've seen them on TV but I was never allowed to go there,' said Todd. 'Security problems.'

'We'll change all that. Now what do you fancy going on?' asked Luke, already heading for the dodgems.

Todd looked surprised. 'Everything, I guess. But . . . but I don't have any cash with me.'

Luke tilted his head. 'Don't worry about that. I've got some. I'll look after you. Come on – let's go.'

Todd didn't need a second invitation. As soon as the dodgems finished their run, he and Luke ran for a car. Damien and Sticky ran for a second car.

'Go ahead, you drive, Todd,' said Luke.

'Gee, thanks,' replied Todd, hopping into the passenger's seat.

'Wrong side,' laughed Luke, as he shoved Todd to the steering wheel. 'We have right-hand drive here, even in the dodgems.'

Todd began to pump the accelerator, trying to rev the engine. As soon as the power was supplied, the car shot away and ploughed into the rear of Sticky and Damien, who were jolted forward. They immediately did a U-turn and took off after Todd's car. They hit it side on. The boys screamed with pure enjoyment. Todd furiously turned the wheel and gave chase. They continued like this until the end of the run.

'Will we go again or would you like to try something else?' Luke asked Todd.

'What's your favourite ride, Luke?' he asked.

'I like the Ghost Train.'

'Let's try that next.'

'We call this the Demon Dart,' Sticky told Todd, as they climbed on board.

Todd enjoyed the ride and wanted to have another go when it had finished. Damien suggested the waltzer instead and they all agreed. This proved exhilarating and the boys stayed on until they began to feel dizzy. From there they tried a variety of the arcade's video games. Todd was an expert.

'You're class at this,' admired Sticky.

'I should be. I play these games all the time back home. What's in there?' asked Todd, pointing towards a door with a sign saying 'Adults Only'.

'Oh you can't go in there. That's where they do the big bets,' explained Luke.

'Come on, let's go somewhere else,' said Sticky.

'You mean there's more?' asked Todd.

'You haven't seen anything yet,' smiled Luke. The boys ran out of the amusements, vaulting over the bollards near the exit.

'That was fantastic. Do you do this all the time?' enquired Todd.

'Not all the time, only when we have the few bob,' said Damien turning his back to count his small change.

'Who's on for a cone?' asked Luke.

Todd was puzzled. 'What's a cone?'

The others burst out laughing. 'He means ice cream, you eejit,' laughed Sticky.

Suddenly realising what he had said and to whom, Sticky quickly apologised. 'I'm sorry, Todd . . . I didn't mean—'

Todd shook his head. 'Don't worry, Sticky, I deserved it. And stop apologising. I'm normal just like you.'

'OK, thanks,' said a red-faced Sticky.

Luke paid for two ice creams, one for himself and the other for Todd. 'Thanks a lot,' said Todd.

'You can get them the next time,' said Luke.

'That's a promise,' replied Todd.

Suddenly Damien pointed towards the promenade. The road train was passing and rang its bell. He ran after it and called to the others.

'Come on quick, everybody after it.'

The four boys ran across the road, dodging in and out between parked cars. Ahead of them the road train was moving slowly along the prom. Damien was first to reach it and grabbed onto one of the seats. The others caught up and Luke hopped onto the runner board. The train came to a halt and the pimply-faced assistant jumped off.

'Get the hell off it,' he yelled.

The boys backed off and stood still for a while. The assistant climbed back on board and the train moved off. Again the boys chased after it and grabbed onto the back. The train jolted to a halt and the irate assistant chased them further up the prom.

Todd was enjoying himself. 'This is cool,' he thought as he stuck out his tongue at the poor assistant.

When the assistant grew purple in the face and began to curse and threaten them, they called a halt to their teasing.

'Hey, lads, we better stop before he gets really mad. Who's on for the bowling alley?' asked Luke.

'Deadly idea, let's get the bikes first,' suggested Damien.

They unchained the bikes and cycled the wrong way up the one-way system on Strand Road. Cars flashed their lights and beeped their horns at them, but the four boys took no notice. Soon they were putting on bowling shoes, having been assigned Lane 5. Damien was first to throw the ball; he only managed to knock down three skittles. Sticky came next and his ball ran into the gulley.

'Are you blind?' scoffed Damien.

'Watch this,' boasted Luke, as he rolled his ball and knocked down six.

'Now its your turn, Todd.'

'I'm not much good at this,' said Todd modestly, but when he rolled the ball he got a full strike.

Some teenage girls in the next lane were giggling and whispering.

'Ignore them. They're always slagging,' said Sticky.

A blonde girl in jeans and a tee shirt blushed as she called to Todd. 'Has anybody ever told you that you look like Todd Harper?'

Todd winked at Luke and put on an Irish accent. 'Wish I was. Everyone says that to me. Are you serious? Do you really think I look like him?'

The girls giggled as the boys laughed.

'If they knew it was really you, they would probably mob you and tear all your clothes off for souvenirs,' grinned Sticky.

Todd drew the baseball cap further down over his eyes. 'Don't go telling anyone. If I'm caught, this is all going to end. And I don't want that to happen. You guys have really shown me a great time.'

Luke shrugged. 'It's OK, we mess about all the time, it's nothing special. Your life must be deadly, though – meeting all the big stars and getting loads of dosh. And flying all over the world. I wouldn't half fancy it.'

Todd frowned. 'But then I have a minder all the time. You've seen how it is. Everything I do is watched closely. I can't go anywhere without an adult. I think this is the first time I've been out with buddies since I got into the movies.'

'But do you not have pals in America?' asked Damien.

He shook his head sadly. 'Not really. The only kids I get to see are my cousins and even then, not very often.'

'That's terrible . . . no friends . . . I wouldn't like that. All on your own.' Damien was sympathetic.

'Does that mean you don't have to go to school?' Sticky liked this idea.

'I don't go to school, but I have a tutor come in, who

goes over all the subjects with me. I've got used to it now.'

Sticky pulled a face. 'That's dire. You mean you have a teacher in your own house? It's bad enough having to go to school but to have a bloody teacher at home – no way!'

'There, you see, it's not all fun,' smiled Todd.

'Would you have lessons and homework and all that sort of rubbish?' asked Damien in disgust.

'Yeah, lots of it and the tutor sometimes comes on location with me. As this is the summer, I don't have him here now,' explained Todd.

Luke shook his head in slow motion. 'And I always thought you movie stars lived a life like in a fairytale.'

'I'd give anything to live a normal life like you guys,' sighed Todd. 'Able to go anywhere and do anything. With nobody on your tail.'

'Would you fancy changing places?' chuckled Sticky.

Todd laughed. 'I wouldn't mind it.'

Luke glanced at his watch. 'Hey lads, its nearly nine thirty. What time will you have to be back, Todd?'

'I guess I should go back to my hotel pretty soon before someone notices. Can you guys show me the way back?' enquired Todd.

'We won't abandon you yet,' Luke assured him as they made their way out of the bowling alley and mounted their bikes. As they raced along the seafront Luke pointed to the Sea Life Aquarium. 'We'll go there the next time.'

'I'm all for that,' replied Todd.

They cycled at speed through the town, over the Dargle bridge and on to Enniskerry. By now the shadows were lengthening and the trees looked spooky. They stood on the pedals as they swung from side to side to push themselves up the hill towards the hotel. Dropping their bikes in the high grass they clambered through the trees.

Todd was first across the lawn and quickly began to climb the ivy. He moved swiftly and soon disappeared through the window. Within seconds he reappeared with David, who seemed sleepy and nervous. David froze as he looked down.

'Come on, man, you'll soon get the hang of it,' said Luke in a loud whisper.

'I . . . I can't . . . is there no other way down?' stuttered David.

'Give over being such a baby. If you don't get a move on, we'll leave you there,' threatened Luke.

'You'll do fine,' said Todd to David, in a comforting voice. 'There's nothing to it. I've been up and down.'

'OK, OK, I'll give it a try,' said David bravely, climbing onto the window ledge. Urged on by Todd from above and Luke from below, he inched his way down the ivy-clad wall. He landed with a thud on the ground.

'Never again, never again.'

'You did grand,' said Sticky. 'Now let's scarper.'

There was no time for any more conversation as they cycled quickly back to their own houses. After all it wouldn't do to have to answer questions if they were late home.

11. Snow in July

Despite being tired, Luke did not sleep much that night. Was it a dream or did they really spend the evening with Todd Harper? Should he tell his parents? Should he tell Barbara? If he told them, they either would not believe him or the news would be all over the town by tomorrow. Todd would be in trouble and they would be kicked off the film. His mind was racing and sleep just would not come.

He was bleary-eyed when his father called him for the second time next morning. He wandered down for breakfast with his eyes half closed.

'Are you feeling all right?' his mother asked with concern.

'Yeah, yeah. Why do you ask?' he replied guiltily.

His mother put her arm around his shoulder. 'It's just that you look as if you haven't slept for a week. Are you sure this film work is not too strenuous for you?'

Luke put on a sudden burst of enthusiasm. 'I'm fine, I'm fine. It's just that I didn't sleep properly. Something was sticking out of the pillow.'

His mother threw her eyes to heaven as she poured his tea. 'I'll have a look at the pillow later.'

'Oh by the way, Luke, you never told us what was in that letter,' his father queried.

'What letter?' asked Luke. 'I got no letter.'

'There was a letter for you yesterday. You mustn't have seen it.'

His mother remarked, 'He ran in and back out of this house like the redcoats were after him yesterday. I never got a chance to even mention it to him.'

'Maybe it's your fan mail,' his father teased.

Luke blushed. 'Don't start so early.'

His father went to the letter rack and returned with a brown envelope which he handed to Luke. He stood beside him as the boy examined the writing.

'Nobody writes to me . . . can't be another school report. Who's it from?' asked Luke.

'You might find out if you opened it,' laughed his father.

'Go way, will you? It might be private,' said Luke, tearing open the envelope.

'Maybe it's from a girlfriend,' winked his mother, 'and he doesn't want us to know.'

'Hey look, it's a cheque,' exclaimed Luke loudly. 'Who'd be sending me a cheque?'

'Show me,' said his mother, taking the cheque and attached note. 'It's from Miss Foot. It's for your work on the film,' she explained. 'Payment for eight days.'

'That's £240,' cheered Luke. 'Will I get that much every week?'

'If you behave yourself, young man, you might,' replied his mother.

'And make sure you put it into your savings account,' declared his father. 'I remember the last time you got a cheque and you squandered it all away on CDs and magazines.'

'Not all of it?' asked Luke in dismay.

'Well you can keep £16 out,' suggested his mother.

Luke appeared disappointed. 'Is that all? A fat lot I'll be able to get with that.'

'You're still working on the film. You could get a lot more before it's finished,' said his father.

'Suppose so,' mumbled Luke.

'This is no hour of the morning to be arguing about money,' sighed his mother.

Their conversation was interrupted with a ring on the hall door.

'That must be your co-stars,' laughed Mr Carroll.

'Bye,' shouted Luke, as he ran to the hall door.

The three boys broke into a sprint down the road as they were running late.

'Wasn't last night brilliant with Todd? He's a regular guy,' said Sticky.

'I'd never have believed he would be so normal. Just like the rest of us,' added Damien, as they raced across the green.

'Now we've got to plan the next move carefully. One false step and we could all be up to our necks in trouble. That includes Todd,' warned Luke.

'What do you think? Any ideas?' asked Sticky.

Luke was thoughtful, 'I think the best thing is to keep our traps shut. Say nothing to anybody. Don't even look at Todd today in case we give the game away.'

'Seems a pity, when he's so nice.'

'We all say nothing, and that's final!' insisted Luke.

Sticky nodded and Damien said 'OK'.

They shook hands on this and then they ran through the studio gate for another day's work. When the boys had changed into their costumes they sat in STAGE C waiting for instructions. Tommy walked briskly to the top of the room and called out, 'Right everybody, outside and onto the bus.'

'Oh no, not up to the bloody bog again,' moaned Sticky.

'There's no use complaining. They're not going to change their minds,' stated Luke as they got onto the bus.

The bus made the first part of the journey at a normal speed but began to shudder as it climbed the Wicklow Mountains. There were spectacular views from the top of the mountain but the boys weren't interested in scenery.

'Hey, am I seeing things or is that really snow,' yelled Sticky, as they drove into the Glen of Imaal.

'Are you losing it? Snow in July,' said Luke, giving him a shove.

Damien sprang to his feet and pointed, 'Look, he's right. It is snow.'

All the boys ran to the right-hand side of the bus and looked out the window. They saw members of the film crew spreading snow with shovels over the side of a hill.

'But where did they get it from? It's too hot for snow,' said Sticky with a puzzled expression.

'They probably have a big fridge that makes it,' said Damien.

'Don't be daft,' said Luke, not sure how they had achieved it but pretending to know.

The bus stopped at the side of the road and the boys quickly filed out. They made a dart for the snow.

Sticky bent down to make a snowball but exclaimed, 'Hey, it's not real snow. It's—' He dropped the mixture of salt and polystyrene.

'You're kidding,' said Luke bending to examine it. 'That's a lousy trick to play on anyone.'

'Get out of there right away,' shouted Tommy through his megaphone.

The boys immediately withdrew from the snow-covered area and bunched together beside the bus. An unhappy Tommy hurried over to address them. 'I'm warning you. Anyone who messes in the snow will be put on the bus and lose a day's pay. Is that understood?'

The boys gave a mixture of nods and mumbles in response.

Before long, a number of limos arrived with Todd, the director and other leading actors. Luke, Sticky and Damien felt uneasy as the new arrivals got out of the cars and walked towards them. Todd winked as he passed by into the snow-covered area. The director waved his arms about as he explained how he wanted the young orphans to play the scene.

A make-up girl passed among the boys, applying a light-coloured make-up. A second girl distributed blankets.

'What are these in aid of?' asked Luke as he examined the scruffy blanket.

'You're suppose to be homeless orphans out in the snow,' explained the girl.

'Did kids really live like this in the olden days?' enquired Damien.

She nodded. 'They were lucky to live to your age. They got very little to eat and wore very thin clothing like what you have now. They didn't have any change of clothes. Times were hard.'

'Janey, that's dire. I'm glad I wasn't around in those days. It's bad enough as it is,' said Damien.

The boys were instructed to put the blankets around their shoulders and to move up hill in a hunched position.

'What on earth is that gadget over there?' asked Sticky nodding towards a wind machine.

'I haven't a clue. Looks like some sort of gigantic fan,' suggested Luke making a guess.

The director stood in front of them and spoke loudly. 'In this scene you are the poor, starving orphans making your way in a snowstorm. I want you to move forward as best you can with your heads down. Look as unhappy and miserable as possible. Somehow I don't think that will be too difficult.'

'That'll be no problem to Damien. Sure he looks miserable all the time,' whispered Luke.

'Ha, ha, very funny,' retorted Damien, not amused.

'Are we all set? . . . Wind machines . . . Snow . . .' called Tommy.

Two large wind machines whirled into action sending a strong breeze and a blizzard of snow towards the boys.

'My God, we'll be blown off the mountain,' moaned Damien as he clutched the blanket tightly around his chest.

'ACTION!' roared the director above the din.

The boys began trudging through the artificial snow and battling against the breeze. They clung together as they genuinely found it difficult to move forward. Stagehands tossed buckets of snow in front of the wind machines. The snow swirled around, the boys catching some in their eyes and mouths.

'Come on . . . faster,' screamed Tommy through his megaphone.

After what seemed like an eternity the director called 'CUT'. The boys stopped dead, coughing and spluttering.

'We'll all have the flu, or worse, after this caper,' said Luke as he wiped snow out of his hair and face.

During the break the boys hopped around, swinging their arms trying to warm themselves up. They didn't have long to recover as the director called them to order.

'This time we're going for real,' he explained. Todd was placed at the top of the group of orphans; the wind machines started again and the call 'ACTION' rang out.

The boys began moving slowly against the wind and snow. Luke noticed Todd a little ahead of him. The young American began staggering, his knees buckled and he fell over. Luke tried to rush forward and pushed some of the others aside. He knelt beside Todd and attempted to assist him to his feet.

'No Luke, no, I'm only acting . . . it's part of the film,' whispered Todd.

Luke froze as the director called 'CUT' in an angry voice. 'Who's that lunatic messing up the scene? Is he trying to ruin my film?'

Tommy rushed to Luke and jerked him to his feet. 'What are you playing at? Do you not understand plain English? You're wasting our time. The scene will have to be re-shot.'

Before he realised it, Luke's face turned crimson as lots of people were shouting at him. It reminded him of school or home. He did his best to explain but nobody wanted to hear. 'But . . . but . . . I didn't . . . ,' he pleaded.

Todd pushed between Tommy and Luke. He glared at Tommy. 'He didn't do any harm. Leave him alone. He thought I was hurt and was helping me. If I made a mistake you wouldn't be bawling me out. Now leave him alone.'

Tommy calmed down, not wanting to upset the star. The director frowned and stated slowly, 'We'll go again and this time nobody go near Todd. Do I make myself understood?'

'Back into first positions,' ordered Tommy.

Luke returned to Sticky and Damien.

'You're a right eejit. What were you thinking of?' enquired Damien.

'You're lucky you didn't get us all chucked off,' snapped Sticky.

'I just thought Todd wasn't well. How was I to know he was acting? Now give over will you,' muttered Luke as he sulked.

'Ah keep your hair on,' replied Damien.

'Quiet everybody. We'll begin the scene again . . . properly this time,' instructed the director in a strict voice.

The scene was repeated, and although it was to the director's satisfaction, it was shot over and over from various angles for the rest of the day.

When they returned to Ardmore Studios at five o'clock all the boys were exhausted. For the first time Luke was too tired to run home. When he reached his house he went in and plopped into an armchair in front of the television. His feet were sore after all the stomping around in the snow, so he took off his shoes and socks.

His mother came in to talk to him. She was surprised by his appearance. 'You look tired. How did it go today? Is it getting to you?'

'You wouldn't believe what they made us do, Mam,' he exclaimed.

'Go on, tell me. I'm sure they were like slave drivers,' said his mother sounding amused.

Luke became animated as he explained. 'They . . . they had us walking through the snow in our bare feet. Then they had a fierce wind blowing. It was like the North Pole. You'd have to see it to believe it. I guarantee you'd swear it was the real thing.'

'You're copping on to the tricks of film making.

You'll be thinking of taking it up full time next,' she suggested.

'No way. Not with all those early starts. Do you think I'm mad?' he replied.

Luke heard the phone ringing in the distance and then heard Barbara answering it. A short time later she burst into the room and announced, 'There's some cheeky little brat with an American accent on the phone for you.'

Luke sat upright and asked, 'How do you mean?'

'Well when I asked him who it was, he said you'd know,' she snorted.

Luke sprang off the armchair and his face brightened. 'Brilliant!'

'Who is it?' demanded Barbara.

Luke didn't answer and hurried out to the phone, closing the door behind him. He whispered into the receiver, 'Is that you Todd?'

'Yeah Luke, sorry I got you into trouble earlier,' he said apologetically.

Luke replied in a friendly tone. 'No, you didn't, Todd. I was daft. I should have known. No harm done. But hey, you're a pretty good actor. You really looked sick.'

Todd laughed. 'It wasn't me. It was the chalky make-up. Makes you look like a corpse.'

Luke continued to speak in a whisper. 'It must be tough doing that sort of thing every day. I don't think I'd fancy it.'

'I've got used to it. Been doing it since I was eight. By the way, thanks for the great time you gave me the other night. I really enjoyed it,' said Todd.

Luke wasn't sure what to say. 'It was great crack all the same . . . and you're all right, you know, ordinary.'

'I only wish I could do it more often,' said Todd sounding a bit disheartened.

'Sure you can. Hey, what about the Tour de France? It comes through Bray next Sunday,' said Luke becoming excited.

'Oh yeah, I heard something about that,' he replied.

'Is there any chance you can get away from your minder to see it?' asked Luke.

Todd hesitated. 'Emm, it's worth a try, but I'm sure we'll be filming on Sunday. That could be a problem.'

'Ah no,' said Luke in a disappointed voice. 'We can't be. We won't even see it ourselves then.'

Todd was thoughtful. 'Tell you what Luke, leave it with me. I'll see if I can swing something. I just might be able to.'

'What are you going to do?' asked Luke curiously.

'I'm saying nothing right now. There's no use building up your hopes,' answered Todd.

The two boys chatted on for a while more about the film and America and life in Bray. Finally Todd told Luke he would ring him again the following evening.

12. Todd's Plan

Over the next few days there was a great buzz of excitement in Bray with the lead up to the Tour de France. Special flags and bunting were erected along Main Street. The shops had lovely colourful window displays relating to all aspects of the Tour de France. One pub even had a penny-farthing bicycle hanging in the window. Throughout the town old photographs of former Bray Wheelers stars could be seen alongside pictures of Stephen Roche and Seán Kelly. They even went so far as to rename Main Street, the 'Champs Elysées'.

Luke, Damien and Sticky were disappointed to miss out on a lot of the fun in the days leading up to the Tour as they were involved with the film. However, they were filming in Ardmore Studios itself, so there was some relief from the discomfort of the bog. A mock street in the period of the 1850s had been constructed alongside one of the stages.

Before filming commenced, the lads wandered in astonishment around the new set. The wooden-fronted buildings had been constructed with attention given to the smallest detail. There was a greengrocer's, an inn, a forge, a dressmaker's and a barber shop, each looking very authentic. The film crew was placing dealers, musicians, beggars and other street people in position. Pigs, sheep, horses and cows were spread out along the street.

'You would swear it was the real thing,' said Luke, his eyes darting from one side to the other.

'Spooky!' said Damien.

Sticky knocked on an artificial wall and got a hollow

response. 'A good puff of wind would blow it all down,' said the ever-sceptical Sticky.

Luke pushed open a door. 'Look at the back of it, its only plywood and canvas. How do they expect to get away with it?'

'Maybe it's only a cheapo film and they can't afford the real thing,' said Damien.

Luke shook his head. 'No way. Not with Todd Harper in it. He's only in brill films.'

'What if we carved our names on a wall, would they see it in the film?' asked Sticky.

Luke gave him a little push. 'Trust you to come up with a hair-brained scheme like that. Do you want to get us all kicked out?'

Suddenly a loud voice barked at them. 'What are you lot playing at? Get back on the set immediately!' Tommy's familiar voice put an end to all their scheming. With their heads bowed, the three boys sheepishly made their way through the bustle back to STAGE C.

Half an hour later the orphans were called on set. For this scene they had to make their way barefooted towards the courthouse through the throngs of people in the busy street. They were to follow Todd, keeping fairly close to him but not so close as to trip anyone up. They did this several times, but it was a tricky scene to get right, especially when one of the horses kicked out and there was a scatter of people. However, everybody worked hard to try to get the actions right and the director praised them all for their efforts.

At lunchtime STAGE C was crowded as all the other extras piled in to be fed. By the time the boys arrived there was a long queue stretching to the door.

'Ah take a look at that. There's no way I'm waiting till they're all served. We'll be here until midnight,' complained Luke.

'But it's a queue, you have to take your turn,' explained Sticky.

With determination in his voice, Luke said, 'Watch me.' He circled around the room and came into view at the top of the queue. He reached in and snatched a lunch bag.

'What the hell do you think you're playing at, sonny?' grumbled a burly man.

'Oh, sorry, sir, my friend's not feeling too good. I've to get something for him to drink,' said Luke, hurrying away.

He sat at the table and was finished his lunch bag by the time Sticky and Damien joined him.

'You're a right chancer, do you know that?' Sticky chuckled.

'Hang on a mo', my fellow orphans, Oliver Twist is going back for more,' Luke giggled as he hurried to the food counter again and returned with another packed lunch.

'We're really going to get the bullet if you keep this up,' said Sticky nervously.

'Does that mean you don't want to share this with me?' asked Luke.

Sticky's stomach overcame his nerves and the three boys enjoyed the extra Mars bars and crisps.

'Hey, what's going on up there?' said Sticky pointing to the top table.

They all turned to see the director climbing on top of the table. He spoke in a booming voice through the megaphone.

'May I have your attention please?'

Gradually a hush fell over the crowd and he spoke again. 'It was our intention to film next Sunday but due to a special request by Todd Harper we will all have the day free. Todd reminded me that for the first time the Tour de France will be passing through Bray and County Wicklow and no doubt you'll all want to see it. So enjoy the day!'

There was a round of applause and loud cheering from the cast and crew.

'Good old Todd,' cheered Luke.

'He must be really important if he can swing something like that,' added Damien.

Sticky held up his ham roll. 'Anyone want to swap a Mars bar for this?'

'Not a chance,' grunted Damien, holding his packed lunch to his chest.

'We've got to plan something with Todd for Sunday. I wonder will he be able to get away?' asked Luke.

'I hope we don't have to get David Nolan again,' moaned Damien.

'Have you got any better ideas?' demanded Luke.

Damien just shrugged.

As the lads returned to the set Todd approached them from behind. He whispered into Luke's ear. 'Don't turn around Luke. Can you come to the hotel early on Sunday morning?'

'No problem. I'll manage it somehow,' mumbled Luke, trying to speak without moving his lips. 'Is there any other way to get in? David won't go up that ivy again.'

'I'll find some other way,' whispered Todd. 'I'll be in touch.' Then he was gone.

When Luke went home after filming that day he told his mother the good news that he would be free to watch the Tour.

'Your Dad's down in the coffee shop hanging up special 'Tour' posters. In fact he might be glad of a helping hand.'

Luke hurried down to the town having told his mother to send Sticky and Damien after him when they called.

In the coffee shop Mr Carroll had lots of colourful posters which had been specially printed by the Tour organisers and local councils that were in the areas the Tour would pass. There was a lovely map of Bray town and his father had put an arrow with 'YOU ARE HERE' written on it pointing to the coffee shop.

'That's deadly,' Luke said to his dad, tracing his finger over the route.

'If you think that's good, wait till you see this,' he said, producing a map of the county with drawings by a famous cartoonist.

Luke was chuffed with the drawings of Saints and Vikings and Romans all riding bicycles around Wicklow. His father interrupted his enthusiastic exclamations.

'Listen, film star, it's a hand I want here. I've a lot of jobs to do to get this place shipshape.'

Luke's pals arrived and they worked in the shop for a while but Sticky soon couldn't resist the temptation to dip his finger into the cream of a meringue. However, Mr Carroll was not too busy to miss this indiscretion.

'Out, the lot of you, out!' he shouted.

The boys were glad to leave and set out to explore the town.

When Luke reached home his mother told him that there had been a telephone call for him and she gave him a number to phone. Luke recognised Todd's number and he immediately rang back.

'Hello, Todd, is everything OK?' he asked when Todd answered the phone.

'Great news, Luke. Great news about Sunday,' Todd was excited.

'Wha . . . what . . . did you find another way in?'

'No – something much better than that! The town council has invited me onto the platform to view the race.'

'That's deadly, Todd!'

'There's more Luke, let me finish. I asked them if I could invite some of my buddies and they agreed! So you, Sticky, Damien, David and your sister, Barbara are all invited to be my guests. What do you think of that?'

Luke was stunned. For one of the few times in his life he was speechless.

'Luke, Luke, are you still there? What do you think, buddy? Do you not like the idea?'

'Are you kidding? It's fantastic. But . . . what will I have to do?' asked Luke.

'Nothing! Just sit there and look important. Don't worry. Gordon and myself will meet you guys on Sunday morning. He's my weekend minder. He will know exactly where to go. Better say goodnight, talk to you in the morning.'

'Can I tell everyone?' asked Luke, still not believing.

Todd replied. 'Why not? Tell your folks. Bye.'

Luke was sitting on the stairs staring at the phone when his mother came into the hallway.

'Have you seen a ghost, Luke? Or fallen asleep?'

He pointed at the phone. 'Todd . . . he told me . . . I'm invited up onto the platform . . .'

'Just start at the beginning. What exactly did he say?'

Luke quickly explained about the invitation from Todd but his mother was a bit sceptical. She initially thought it might be one of Luke's tall tales but after a while was convinced and was pleased. Luke heard her telling his father when he came home and they talked about the great honour late into the night. Barbara asked if she was included in the invitation. Finally, after stalling a good deal Luke told her she was.

The last thing Luke heard before he fell asleep was his mother saying, 'I'd better organise some clean clothes for you. We can't have you making a holy show of us in front of the whole town where your ancestors have lived since Adam was a highlander.'

13. Tour de France

Luke was woken at seven o'clock on Sunday by unusual sounds outside his house. He bounded out of bed and looked out of the window. Huge forty-foot trucks were off-loading crash barriers at the side of the road. Men were climbing up ladders and onto the roofs of vans attaching banners and signs on all the lampposts.

'My God, it's started already?' he cried, as he charged down the stairs and into the kitchen. His parents were sitting at the table eating their breakfast.

'Slow down, Luke, you're not competing in the Tour. You'll blow a fuse.'

'But, but everyone's outside, it's all happening,' he exclaimed.

'They're the support crews making preparations. The race won't pass this way for hours,' explained his father. 'You have loads of time to have your breakfast and get yourself cleaned up.'

'That's OK then; I was worried there for a minute,' said Luke, as he poured himself a cup of tea and sat down at the table.

Barbara ran into the kitchen yelling, 'Look out the front window. Quick! You'll never believe your eyes.'

Her mother tried to calm her down. 'It's only the trucks for the Tour, Barbara, they've been busy for the last hour or more.'

'No, not that, there's a huge car outside our house. Honest.'

They all went into the sitting room and Barbara drew back the corner of the curtain for them to peep out. Luke

112

was speechless with surprise. Barbara was right, a long back limousine was parking outside their house. More surprising still was that Gordon, Todd's minder, was coming up their garden path.

'What's does he want with us? I hope there's nothing wrong with Todd.'

But his fears were soon allayed when he noticed Todd hopping out of the back door of the car.

'Look who it is . . . it's Todd Harper coming to our house,' said Barbara in disbelief.

Luke brushed past his parents and headed out to the hall door. The whole family was behind him by the time he got the door open. Todd and Gordon were standing in the porch.

Luke was flustered by the actor's arrival, but he remembered his manners and introduced his parents.

'This is my Mam and Dad . . . '

'Very pleased to meet you,' Todd replied to their greetings.

Gordon was equally as polite; he showed beautiful white shining teeth as he smiled broadly. Barbara pushed herself forward.

'I'm Barbara.' Luke knew he would be in trouble for omitting her.

'Oh you must be Luke's pretty sister,' Todd said, ever the gentleman.

Luke said, 'I wouldn't go that far.'

Mrs Carroll asked, 'Would you like to come in?'

'Thank you but we've come to invite Luke and Barbara to McDonald's for breakfast,' said Todd.

'Yes, yes, that would be great,' replied Luke.

'Fantastic!' exclaimed Barbara.

'It would be a good idea if you got dressed first,' smiled their father.

They all laughed.

'Give me ten seconds,' said Luke, racing up the stairs.

Barbara also ran to get dressed while Mr and Mrs Carroll led Todd and Gordon into the sitting room. Within minutes Luke and Barbara returned to find them all chatting and laughing.

Mr Carroll was talking to Gordon. 'I suggest you leave your car at the house here, you might have trouble getting parking in Main Street.'

'Good idea,' replied Gordon. 'We've already telephoned your buddies to meet us there,' he explained to Luke.

Gordon seemed to be a good organiser; there was obviously more to being a minder than Luke had first thought.

His parents declined the invitation to join them.

'Trust our Luke to swing something like that,' Mr Carroll remarked to his wife as he watched them striding down the road.

When they entered McDonalds, Sticky and Damien were already there. David Nolan was there too. Todd led the lads to a table saying, 'Gordon knows what we like, he'll order for us.' They were not disappointed when Gordon came back laden with all sorts of burgers, fries and drinks.

By the time they emerged into the daylight, crowds were converging on Main Street. Families were gathering behind crash barriers on either side of the street. Almost every child was carrying French or Irish flags.

The Gig Rig, a large truck with two rows of chairs

arranged on top, was placed close to the Town Hall – this was to be the viewing platform. Men in neat suits and women in summer dresses were climbing up the steps to the platform.

'That must be where we are to sit,' Todd remarked as they made their way towards the platform.

The chairman of the town council stepped forward to greet them. He was wearing a chain of office around his neck. He held out his hand and smiled, 'Young Mister Harper, you're very welcome.'

Todd shook hands with him. 'Thank you very much for inviting us, Mr Collins.'

'It's our pleasure, Todd, we are only too delighted to have you and your friend with us today. I hope you are enjoying your stay in Bray,' said Mr Collins as he took Todd by the elbow and led him towards the platform. Gordon followed behind.

Todd turned round. 'Hey hang on, my buddies are coming too.'

The chairman glared at the boys and Barbara and then cocked his head. The children quickly followed Todd and Gordon onto the stand.

Todd sat beside the chairman. Luke, Sticky and Damien jumped onto three adjoining chairs. David and Barbara stood to one side. The other VIPs stood in a huddle behind them; they were not impressed with the boys occupying the last few free seats.

Luke felt chuffed to be sitting among the dignitaries who included the parish priest, TDs, other councillors and several local business people. The boys whistled and catcalled when any of their friends passed by the stand. The people on the platform glared and frowned at the boys' behaviour. Luke blushed when he saw his parents passing on the far side of the road. His mother smiled and waved.

Luke was soon bored with waiting for the Tour to start and looked around for something to amuse himself. He enjoyed pranks and felt that this was a good opportunity to play one. A woman sitting in front of him had a floral dress with a long bow hanging down the back. He glanced around to make sure that nobody was watching as he took the end of the ribbon and tied it to the leg of a chair.

Soon the fun began and the brass band struck up. A loudspeaker gave an update on the event and announced that the Tour de France had officially left Dublin. Within minutes the cavalcade consisting of race officials, media personnel and hordes of vehicles came careering up Main Street. These were followed by an assortment of advertising cars for the cycling companies. Some of the cars were very amusing and original. A loud cheer went up when a convoy of French and Irish motorcycle police went by. Soon the loudspeaker announced that the race itself was on the outskirts of Bray and was entering the roundabout at Woodbrook.

'This should be brill,' said Luke, leaning forward on his chair.

'Did you ever see it before, Todd?' enquired Damien.

Todd shook his head. 'No, only on TV. It sure looks like hard work.'

Mr Collins leaned over and explained that there was to be a sprint finish about a hundred metres beyond the Town Hall. Before he had finished speaking, the 189 tanned cyclists in twenty-one different coloured team jerseys sped up Main Street. The roar of the support motorcycles and the overhead helicopters drowned out the cheering and clapping of the crowd. Many of the riders stood up on their pedals to put on an extra spurt for the sprint finish and the extra points on offer.

The cyclists were gone as quickly as they had come. Support teams with spare bicycles and bicycle parts whizzed by and a fleet of ambulances followed them. Immediately after the race had cleared the town, teams of workmen moved in to dismantle the barriers and remove the signs.

'Is that all?' asked Luke looking down the street hoping to see more.

'Looks like it, buddy,' grinned Todd. 'These guys don't hang around.'

The chairman spoke to them. 'I'd say they're half way to Wicklow by now.'

The dignitaries then began to stand up, including the woman in the floral dress. There was a loud rip as the back of her dress tore away, exposing her underwear. Her face was bright red as she grabbed her dress and held it to her back.

The children including Todd burst into a fit of giggles.

'Are you responsible for this?' the chairman demanded, frowning angrily at them.

'Who, me?' asked Luke in an innocent voice.

'How dare you! My buddy had nothing to do with that woman's accident,' stated Todd loudly.

'I didn't mean—' began the chairman becoming embarrassed as people looked on.

Some of the other dignitaries held coats around the distraught woman and escorted her away.

'Thank you very much for everything. We're leaving now,' said Todd as he moved towards the steps.

'But we were going to invite you to—' said the chairman, cutting short his sentence.

Todd and the other children left the viewing stand. When they were out of range Todd leaned over and whispered, 'That was a neat trick, Luke.'

'You mean you . . .?' said Luke with surprise.

Todd quickly put his finger to his lips and muttered, 'Shush.'

They were joined by Gordon who asked, 'Where to now, boss?'

'Emm . . . let's see,' said Todd thoughtfully. 'What would you guys say to going to lunch at my hotel?'

'Brill,' replied Luke. 'You can count me in.'

'And the rest of you?' enquired Todd, turning to face the others.

'But I have to meet my friends,' said Barbara, sounding disappointed.

'We'd love to have you along,' said Todd touching her on the arm.

'Ok then I'll go,' smiled Barbara feeling chuffed.

Everybody else was enthusiastic about the invitation and accepted. They walked up to Luke's house to collect the limo. As they all clambered into the car, Luke's mother came out to speak to them. She stood staring at the car in astonishment.

Gordon rolled down the rear window and Luke popped his head out. He put on a posh accent. 'Mother dear, I'm afraid we won't be dining at home today. Master Todd Harper has invited us for luncheon.'

Mrs Carroll was so surprised that she could hardly speak. Finally she said, 'Do you lot not want to get cleaned up first?'

Todd grinned out at her, 'They're fine as they are, Mrs Carroll. We'll drop them back later. Good luck.'

Gordon had difficulty driving the car out of the estate as dozens of children had gathered around to see the stretch limo and Todd Harper. Mrs Carroll was still standing with her mouth open as the car drove off up Killarney Road.

Luke was disappointed that the windows were darkened. He could see out but nobody could see in. They passed by some of his schoolfriends and football pals who stared and pointed at the car. This was the life, thought Luke. He could live like this all the time.

Soon they were at the hotel. Gordon opened the doors to allow everyone out. Luke, Damien, Sticky, Barbara and David felt nervous as they entered. Todd led them across the plush lobby to the dining room. There were diners at about half the tables. The room was set out formally with wine glasses and silver cutlery arranged on white tablecloths. A waiter in a dress suit showed them to their table.

Clumsily the boys sat down. Only Todd seemed relaxed. Luke inspected the array of knives, forks and spoons before him.

'Hey, they gave us too many. I'll only need one,' announced Luke.

'Half the time at home you only use your fingers,' remarked Barbara.

Todd began to laugh.

'What's up?' asked a puzzled Luke.

Todd held his hand to his mouth to prevent himself laughing. 'I guarantee you'll need them all.'

The waiter nodded as he handed each of them a menu.

Luke's mouth fell open. There were so many choices. He didn't have to look at the menu in McDonalds. He knew exactly what he wanted. He leaned over to Todd, 'All I want is a burger and chips or chicken and chips.'

'Me too,' added David, delighted to be in the thick of it.

'You're kidding me. You'll have to eat more than that. Can I order for you all?' enquired Todd.

'Fire away,' replied Luke, handing him the menu.

'And the rest of you?' asked Todd.

They all agreed.

'I'll order my own favourite,' said Todd beckoning the waiter. He ordered French onion soup, sirloin steak and chips and Coke for everyone. Barbara and the boys were not disappointed with his choice and tucked into the food. They waited until Todd began to eat to see which cutlery he was using.

The children quickly forgot the formalities and tucked into the meal.

'You seem to be enjoying it,' commented Todd as he glanced from face to face to judge their reactions.

'This is deadly. I could eat this every day,' replied Luke with his mouth full.

Sticky licked his fingers as he shoved the last of the chips into his mouth. He mumbled but nobody could understand him.

'Who's for more chips?' asked Todd.

Sticky nodded. The others all asked for more. When they had consumed the extra chips it was desserts all round. They finished off the meal with two cups of coffee each. As he drank the last of his coffee, Damien gave a loud belch. The others tittered, as he grew embarrassed. The people at the next table glared at him.

'All full?' enquired Todd as the waiter began removing the plates.

'Wow, that was something else,' announced Sticky, patting his full stomach.

'That was wonderful,' said Barbara.

'I wouldn't half fancy that every day,' added Damien.

'You'd soon get tired of it,' said Todd sounding a little despondent.

'Thanks a million, Todd. Do you want us to pay for it?' asked Luke, unsure how to react.

'No way! It's the least I could do after the kindness you've shown me. I wouldn't mind changing places with you,' said Todd as his eyes began to moisten.

Luke ruffled his hair. 'You must be losing it, Todd. You'd give up your great life for our ordinary one?'

'You guys have freedom. You can go where you like, say what you like, talk to anyone you like. I have none of that. Being a big film star isn't everything. I enjoy things like hanging out and playing football and bowling. That's real life,' he explained, sounding sad.

Luke gave a deep sigh, feeling sorry for his friend. Their conversation was disturbed by the arrival of Gordon at their table. 'Sorry to disturb you, Todd, but your mom and dad are on the phone.'

'Oh great,' replied Todd springing to his feet. 'Sorry guys, but I'll have to go. Gordon will run you back home.'

With that Todd hurried from the dining room. Gordon stood beside the table smiling. 'When you're ready, I'll give you a lift back to Bray.'

The children didn't need a second invitation and headed for the car park. They felt like royalty as they travelled home in the stretch limo.

14. The Party

It wasn't long until filming neared completion. Word spread through the cast and crew that this would be the last week's work on the film. Although Luke and his pals had complained at the beginning of the tough conditions they had to endure, they had grown used to it. They were going to miss the big adventure. They were never going to experience the likes of this again in their lives.

One day at lunchtime Tommy addressed the extras as they ate their lunch. 'I would like to inform you all that the wrap party will take place in the studio next Friday night. You are all welcome to come along.'

Luke appeared confused.

'What on earth is a wrap party?' asked Damien.

Sticky shrugged. 'Beats me. Maybe you have to wrap something around yourself or something.'

'There's one way of finding out,' said Luke. He made a funnel of his hands and held them to his mouth. 'Tell us, what's a wrap party?' he yelled at Tommy.

Tommy pulled a face and replied, 'That's what they call the party at the end of a film.'

Luke scratched his head and said, 'Thanks.'

'Daft name to call a party,' remarked Damien.

'It's a pity it's all going to be over soon. The whole thing was a bit of gas,' said Sticky, finishing his Mars bar.

'I wonder what the chances are of us getting into another film?' enquired Damien.

Luke frowned. 'If it means going to Miss Flippin' Foot every week – no way. Nothing is worth that. All her talking posh and poems.'

'We mightn't have to. Maybe when the film is shown in America they'll want us to be in other ones like Todd is,' said Sticky enthusiastically.

Luke belted him on the head with his roll. 'What sort of eejit are you? You've got a better chance of winning a million on the lottery than that.'

Sticky frowned. 'Ah, give over. It was only an idea.'

'Do you think Todd will say goodbye to us?' enquired Damien.

'I'm dead sure he will. He's OK. I wonder will he ever come back to Bray, though,' said Luke, thinking out loud.

The boys didn't have long to wait before Todd was in touch. During the afternoon he passed a note to Luke. It read: *Luke, in case I don't get to talk to you at the party, would you and your buddies like to call up to my hotel on Saturday morning. I want to say goodbye. I will be flying home in the afternoon. Todd.*

Luke passed the note around to Sticky and Damien. It gave them a lift but also made them feel a bit sad.

Friday came around quickly. When filming finished, the boys handed in their ragged clothes for the last time. They were told that the wrap party would start at eight o'clock. Luke sprinted home and had a quick shower. His mother had his best clothes laid out on the bed. He quickly changed into them.

As the family sat at the table, Luke's mother began giving him advice. 'Now Luke, I want to give you a few tips. For starters make sure you don't touch a drop of alcohol.'

Luke sighed. 'What do you take me for?'

'Don't bite my nose off. I just want you to be sensible.

You've never been at anything like this before,' she advised.

Luke didn't feel in the humour for a sermon. 'But there'll be dozens of other lads too.'

'And if anyone offers you anything, don't take it,' warned his mother.

'Does that go for food too?' responded Luke sarcastically.

His mother's voice became louder. 'You know exactly what I mean, young man. Any more of your lip and you won't go at all.'

Luke thought it best to behave himself and just listen to the advice. When Damien and Sticky arrived at his house his mother drove them all to the studio. She continued to lecture them on the journey. As she parked at the studio gate she said, 'Now remember, be on your best behaviour. No messing around. When the party's over give me a ring and I'll come up and collect you.'

The boys sprang from the car and entered the gate without listening to a single word she was saying.

When they entered STAGE C they found it completely transformed. There were flashing disco lights and a band, consisting of two middle-aged men, wearing cowboy hats, was playing on a small stage. One was on a keyboard, the other on a guitar. On either side of the room two long tables were set out. One had a buffet with turkey, ham, salmon, salads, pavlovas, Black Forest gateaux and cheesecakes. The other table had an array of drinks and minerals.

'Would you take a look at that,' said Sticky with glee, as he headed for the food table. He immediately grabbed a plate and soon had it filled to capacity.

The other two lads followed him and layered their plates with turkey and ham. They sat side by side against the wall and quickly began eating.

Tommy stepped up to the microphone and began to compere the evening. He encouraged people to dance. Luke, Sticky and Damien hopped onto the floor and began to display their disco steps. Some of the actors and crew went up on the stage and sang their party pieces.

'Come on, are you on?' called Luke to his pals.

'Yeah, why not? Let's go,' replied Sticky as they headed for the stage.

Luke grabbed the microphone and burst into Boyzone's 'When the Going Gets Tough'. Damien and Sticky joined in and the band accompanied them. They danced about the stage.

Suddenly Luke realised that a fourth boy had joined them. He glanced over his shoulder to discover that it was Todd Harper. The young American sang and danced with them. When they finished the song they were cheered and applauded by the crowd. There were shouts for Todd to sing another song.

Todd smiled and spoke to the musicians. Then he burst into singing and dancing to 'Singing in the Rain'.

The boys really enjoyed the atmosphere of the night. In between dancing they moved from the mineral bar to the dessert table, stuffing themselves. By the end of the night they were absolutely full. Their only complaint was that they didn't get an opportunity to talk to Todd.

At half past twelve Luke decided it was time to call it a night. He rang his mother from a payphone. Ten minutes later she arrived at the studio. On the way home, Luke told her all about the fun he'd had singing with Todd on stage.

He was up most of the night with cramps in his stomach from all he had eaten. Mid-morning the next day, Luke crawled out of bed bleary-eyed and only drank water for his breakfast. He waited until Sticky and Damien arrived and then they cycled at a gentle pace to Todd's hotel. They felt a mixture of excitement and sadness as they were going to see Todd for the last time. Each of their parents had given them a small present for Todd.

As they cycled up the driveway they spotted Todd and Gordon kicking a ball in front of the hotel.

On hearing them approach Todd turned and greeted them, 'Hi lads, glad you made it in time.'

'What time are you leaving?' asked Luke.

'Shortly. I have to catch a flight early afternoon,' explained Todd. He gestured to Gordon and his minder turned and went into the hotel.

'Tell us Todd, did you like it here?' asked Damien as they dismounted and dropped their bikes on the grass.

'Sure,' replied Todd sitting down. 'I'm sorry I didn't get more free time. I really enjoyed myself with you guys.'

'It was deadly for us too,' said Luke sitting beside him.

Gordon returned with an armful of gifts and a camera dangling around his neck. 'Here you go.'

'Thanks Gordon,' said Todd, taking the presents and checking the names on the tags. 'Damien, this is for you,' he said as he handed him a present.

'Oh thanks!' exclaimed Damien.

Todd then passed a parcel each to Luke and Sticky.

'Can we open them now?' asked Luke excitedly.

'Sure thing. They're no good to you wrapped up,' laughed Todd.

The boys quickly tore off the wrapping paper. They each had been given a top-of-the-range playstation.

'Wow! It's a playstation,' yelled Luke.

'But they cost a mint,' added Damien.

Sticky opened his mouth and closed it several times before he could speak. Finally he said, 'It's what I always wanted.'

Todd appeared pleased. 'Glad you like them. I wasn't sure what to get. I have one here for David. Can you pass it on?'

'Sure, Todd,' said Damien, taking the parcel from him.

Luke took his present from the carrier on his bike and gave it to Todd. 'This is a small thing,' he muttered, feeling embarrassed with Todd's expensive present.

Todd unwrapped it to discover a tee shirt with the words 'I'll Never Forget Bray' written across a picture of Bray Head. 'Hey, I like it. It'll remind me of my visit.'

Damien presented him with a book *The History of Bray*. Todd tried to appear interested but he wasn't. He took more of a liking to Sticky's present, another book, *Irish Film: 100 Years*.

'I'll really enjoy this one,' said Todd, flicking through the pages. 'I never realised there were so many movies made in Ireland.'

'Eh, don't blame me about the book,' said Damien, slightly embarrassed. 'It wasn't my idea. It was my mother's. She's into books big time.'

'Aren't they all?' began Todd and then burst out laughing. 'Don't worry about it.'

'I wonder when *Orphans' Retreat* will be on in the Royal?' enquired Luke.

'Probably not till this time next year,' replied Todd.

'You're having me on. Sure it's finished and all,' said Luke disbelieving.

Todd smiled. 'The actual film yes but not the editing or soundtrack or dubbing and so on.'

'Hey Todd,' came a shout from Gordon, standing beside the stretch limo. He was pointing to his watch.

'I'm afraid it's time to go,' said Todd, trying to fake a smile. 'You never know, we might meet again.' Todd held out his hand.

'Let's hope so,' replied Luke nervously chewing his lower lip. He stretched out his hand to shake Todd's.

They shook hands warmly. Without saying another word Todd walked across the gravel to the limo. Gordon opened the rear door and allowed him in. Before Todd closed the door he waved at the three boys. They waved back. Then the door slammed closed. The engine started and the limo drove slowly down the driveway. The boys kept watching until the car was out of sight.

Sticky was first to speak. 'Was that all a dream or did it really happen?'

'It was no dream and it won't ever happen again,' said Luke quietly.

'And these playstations. They cost a bomb,' said Damien, closely examining his present.

Sticky nodded. 'I wonder will we ever see him again?'

'You never know. He might come back some day to make another film,' said Damien, sounding more positive.

'He might,' added Sticky.

'Come on, let's blow. Last one back to the den is an idiot,' said Luke, running towards the bikes.